Old Flames

A NORTHWEST MAGIC NOVEL

Old Flames

ELISA KEYSTON

Crimson Fox
PUBLISHING

TURNER, OREGON

For Jane

Two years before the events of Alexandra's Riddle...

Chapter 1

Laney McCarthy was not pleased.

She scowled, adjusting the puffed sleeves of the brocade jacket on the dress form while raging silently in her head. She was more than just displeased, actually. She was, as her dad would say, *hopping mad*. So angry, in fact, that she couldn't even decide who was most deserving of her wrath. Her mind was a whirl of thoughts, the jumbled panic caused by this morning's email serving only to fan the flames of her notoriously volatile temper.

The network was the obvious first choice to take the blame; if they'd told Laney weeks ago who was coming to do the interview, she never would have agreed to participate in the segment. She wouldn't have even set foot on the museum grounds today. She'd be hiding out at home, ordering takeout and not leaving the safety of her apartment until the news crew had long since departed.

Of course, it was entirely possible that they *had* told Viv and she'd neglected to pass the information along. As the museum director, Viv had done most of the coordinating for the feature. It probably wouldn't have occurred to her to warn Laney about the reporter who was coming to Foreston to do the interview. Why would it matter? She couldn't possibly have known Laney's personal reasons for wanting to avoid one particular member of the network's staff—especially since Laney had kept that facet of her history pretty close to the chest.

She gnawed her lip in annoyance. She supposed she could still blame the network for employing him in the first place, though that was also a stretch.

No, the one most deserving of her ire, Laney decided, was Diane. Because Diane *did* know their history, now. And she'd still told Laney that it was her own problem, just like the crotchety old bat she was…

"What's that face about?" asked Carmen, one of the other museum docents, passing through the parlor on her way to the formal dining room. She struggled under the weight of a large cardboard box labeled *Tea Settings*.

"It's nothing," Laney said, grabbing a garment brush off the velvet chair beside her and attacking the brocade jacket with it.

"Oh, right, nothing," Carmen snorted. "I just hope you

weren't making that face when you sewed that costume, or whoever buys it at the auction tomorrow is going to be sorry."

Laney scowled. If there was one thing she couldn't stand, it was people being reasonable when she was busy flying off the handle. "Come on, Carmen," she sniffed.

Carmen braced the box she'd been carrying against her hip and wiped her sweaty forehead with the back of her hand. It was over ninety degrees outside, and since the museum lacked air conditioning, it was oppressively stuffy inside, even with the windows open. "No, you come on, Laney," she said with a wry quirk of her eyebrow. "I've heard the story about your brother's band uniform enough times to know what happens when you sew while cranky." As Laney's glare deepened, Carmen burst into laughter. "Fine, be that way," she said, carrying the box of tea settings through the parlor door. "I'm just saying, if you were in a mood when you made that dress, we better throw it out right now."

Laney ignored her, giving the costume one last once-over. It was a period outfit, a Victorian lady's dress in a rich burgundy hue with a brocade jacket to match. When she lifted the sleeves, she noticed a small hole in the right armpit where a few stitches had come undone. She moved back to the velvet chair, rummaging through her sewing kit. As she threaded a needle, she took a few deep breaths and tried to calm her temper. As much as she didn't want to admit it right now—as much as she wanted to pretend that her mood had had nothing to do with Matthew's broken leg, or what had happened to the girl who bought that Renaissance bodice, or any of the other strange things that had happened to people who wore clothes Laney had made—she knew better than that. And Carmen was right; whoever eventually wound up wearing this dress didn't deserve whatever fate Laney's temper might be imbuing into it right now.

Besides, angry stitches were uneven stitches.

When she'd managed to calm herself from a boiling rage to a firm neutral (genuine pleasantness was going to be impossible today), she removed the jacket from the dress form, turning the sleeve inside out. Then she pushed the needle through the stiff fabric, back and forth, forcing her hand to remain steady and her stitches to remain small. When the repair was done, she stepped back, looking the ensemble over again. Satisfied, she left the parlor and headed down the hall to help Carmen with the table settings.

"There," Carmen said with a smile as Laney came into the dining room. "Feeling better?" She stood beside the massive oak table, a salad fork in her hand. The table was mostly set now in the standard Victorian high tea formation, though Carmen had used the museum's display china today instead of the cheaper pieces they used for the monthly catered tea events. Usually the actual antique china only saw the light of day during the holiday open house, but they wanted the house to look extra nice today.

After all, the Paine Estate was going to be on the news. And not just the local news, or the public access channel—they'd scored a coveted slot on a national cable news series' weekly *Around America* segment. All the other destinations that had been featured in the segment had seen a massive spike in tourism for months afterward, and with the holiday season coming up in just a few months, it was the perfect opportunity not just for the Paine Estate, but for the entire town of Foreston, Washington to bring in some much-needed tourist revenue.

All the volunteer docents at the Victorian house museum had been delighted when they'd gotten the call, but Laney had been extra proud. The network wanted to schedule the interview to coincide with the Paine Estate's annual fashion show and silent auction, an event that Laney herself had spearheaded two years ago and had organized every year since. She actually made many of the period outfits that were shown off on the runway and then auctioned, and coordinated with vintage shops and department stores—and even a couple designers in the Portland area—to donate items to the fundraiser. This year's fashion show was shaping up to be their biggest yet, and Laney had been over the moon that it was going to get coverage on national television.

The only problem was the person the network had assigned to do the interview. Usually the *Around America* segment was hosted by Gloria Shellburg, but this morning Laney had learned that the pleasant middle-aged woman was not the person the network had decided to send after all. Instead, they'd sent—

Laney's phone buzzed in her pocket. Deciding that this would be a welcome distraction from answering Carmen's question, she half-turned and pulled her phone out.

It took everything in her not to hurl the phone across the room when she saw the text on the lock screen, though. It was from her sister, Taryn:

Look who I just saw on Main Street. Did you know he was coming here??

A photo was attached of a tall, fit young man with sandy brown hair. He wore a gray T-shirt, the kind plain and simple enough that he probably didn't think anything of it when he threw it on, but which accentuated his muscular build in all the right places. He was wearing sunglasses, but Laney knew all too well that the sparkling blue eyes underneath them were the same color as the sky.

It had been years since she'd seen him anywhere but the TV— and even then, only long enough to find the remote and change the channel—but Laney could tell that time had done nothing to dull Paul's good looks. If this photo was any indication, he'd only gotten *more* handsome.

She looked up from her phone to Carmen, who was watching her with her brows raised. "No," she said. "I am most definitely not feeling better."

Chapter 2

"Wait a minute," Carmen said, still trying to process the information Laney had just given her. "You're telling me you used to date Paul Nelson? The British guy from the news?"

"Yup," Laney said, keeping her eyes firmly riveted on the place setting in front of her: A gold charger with a luncheon plate, a bread plate to the upper left of that with a spreader atop it, teacup and saucer, two forks (salad and dinner), dinner knife, and two spoons (soup and tea). Perfect. "For about a year, in college."

"College?" Carmen seemed to count backward in her head for a moment, to when Laney would have been that age. "Was that when he was a uVer?"

Laney nodded. uView was a popular video-sharing platform, and Paul had started his channel on world news and political commentary when he was a teenager, but he hadn't started to get popular until he and Laney were dating. His subscriber count had shot up during the last few months she'd been in London—her third year of college—when he'd finally saved up enough of the ad revenue he was earning from his videos to buy a high-quality camera and everyone had finally noticed, in glorious 4K resolution, just how handsome this offbeat alternative journalist actually was.

"Wow," Carmen breathed. "I had no idea."

"I don't like to talk about it."

Carmen frowned but didn't press it, which Laney appreciated. It was bad enough that she'd had to go through it all with Diane. Carmen was a good friend, and had been ever since she and her husband Josh had moved to the area the year before and Carmen had started volunteering at the Paine Estate Museum. But the subject of Paul Nelson—of everything about that wonderful year studying abroad and the horrible way it had ended—was not one that Laney enjoyed reliving, no matter how sympathetic the audience.

"Did you know he was the one coming out here to do the interview?" Carmen asked.

"Nope. I figured it would be Gloria Shellburg. I guess I just assumed. Viv said someone from the network would be coming out this week, but she didn't say who." The museum director, Vivian Schmidt, was one of only three paid staff at the Paine Estate. Since the house and grounds were owned by the city and managed by a small nonprofit, the museum operated on a next-to-nonexistent budget, which meant that most of the docents, like Laney, were volunteers. But Viv was on vacation, taking a two-week cruise to Mexico with her husband for their twenty-fifth wedding anniversary.

"Well, can't Diane do it?" Carmen's voice dropped to a whisper as she glanced back in the direction of Diane's office.

"Yeah, you'd think," Laney whispered back. Diane Mackechnie, another member of the staff, was the self-proclaimed second-in-command at the Paine Estate. As event coordinator, her official job was to handle private rentals and functions like the museum's monthly high teas, but she managed to butt into just about every other function in the museum's operations—much to the consternation of Viv and Suze, the museum's collections manager and the third paid staffer. Diane had an infuriating way of being nosy about everything, but simultaneously being dismissive of everything. Just as she had been when Laney had knocked on her office door this morning to explain the situation. When Laney had seen Paul's name on the email that all the volunteers had been sent this morning, she'd asked Diane if she'd be willing to step in and do the interview in her place.

That hadn't exactly gone well.

"She just told me, 'Your event, your gig,'" Laney said glumly.

"What, her desire to spite you overpowered her need to be the center of attention?" Carmen rolled her eyes. "She must really be salty about the fashion show."

"Please," Laney muttered. "That woman is saltier than the Dead Sea."

"I know she's frustrated that she has to give up a weekend in peak wedding season so the museum can host the fashion show, but come on! It's just *one* weekend," Carmen pointed out. "And the fashion show raises about as much money for the museum foundation as a rental does, anyway, right?"

"Last year it did. And this year's looking like it will be bigger," Laney said. "Not to mention that this is better for the community than a private rental is." She tried not to wince as she remembered Diane's response the last time Laney had mentioned that fact: *"And even better for your shop, isn't it?"*

Carmen put a knowing hand on Laney's shoulder. She'd been there when Diane made that remark, and she knew that it bothered Laney that Diane had implied that she would put her own business in front of the museum's welfare. "Don't let old sourpuss get you down," Carmen said kindly. "She's just jealous that she didn't come up with the idea herself. You know how she likes to micromanage everything. It probably drives her crazy that there's an event at the museum that she's not in charge of."

"Yeah," Laney said, tucking a lock of her red hair behind her ear self-consciously.

"Anyway, what about Suze? Can she do the interview for you?" Carmen suggested.

Laney shook her head. "She's in Portland for that conference, remember? She's staying overnight with her sister and driving back tomorrow morning."

Carmen hesitated a moment before asking, her brows furrowed, "Do you want me to do the interview, Laney? I know I haven't been here that long, but..." She trailed off, then forced a smile and said, "I think I could do it."

Laney smiled back appreciatively. She could see the anxiety all over her friend's face, the way her tan skin had blanched—not just because she wasn't as familiar with the fashion show as Laney was, but also at the thought of appearing on national television. Carmen was quiet and reserved; Laney couldn't make her push herself out of her comfort zone just so she could avoid talking to her ex-boyfriend. "It's all right. Thank you for offering," she said. "Diane's right. It's my event, my gig. I can manage Paul. Honestly."

The relief on Carmen's face was obvious, even as she asked, "Are you sure?"

"Yeah, I'm sure. I haven't even seen the guy in person in five years. That was practically a lifetime ago. It might be a little awkward, but it will be fine."

Carmen nodded reassuringly. "And we can laugh about it when it's over."

"Exactly," Laney agreed, even though she didn't feel very convinced. She couldn't see herself laughing about what had happened with Paul any time soon, and she doubted this visit would do much to help that. Even now, after all these years, her stomach still knotted up as she remembered that night in the pub...

Seeing him with *her*.

And then what had happened after.

She shook her head, trying to clear it as her eyes started to sting once more. *No.* She wasn't going to think about it. She was going to be cool, indifferent when she saw him. She was a successful career woman. When her parents had retired from their clothing alteration shop two years ago, she'd taken over the business, and she was doing pretty well if she said so herself. Better than one would expect for a small-town tailor. The rumors about her *magic touch*, as the locals referred to it, had brought in a lot of business, from as far east as the Tri-Cities to as far north as Olympia. And volunteering at the museum took up most of her free time. She was successful, busy, and fulfilled.

Professionally, anyway.

She sighed quietly, taking a step back and looking at the finished table settings. The light from the overhead chandelier made the china and silver on the table sparkle with an almost otherworldly quality.

"The silver looks really nice," she commented to Carmen. "Did you polish it this morning?"

Carmen shook her head. "Came out of the box that way. The whole house looks really nice, honestly. Think the brownies were here?"

Laney glanced around the room. She didn't see anything, but that was typical for her. If Taryn were here, she'd be able to say for sure. Laney just shrugged. "Wouldn't put it past them. They probably sensed that something big was happening, and you know they love to be helpful. Better make sure we leave something out for them tonight, just in case."

Carmen nodded. A year ago she'd laughed incredulously at the town legend that the Paine Estate was inhabited by fae, but after spending a year in Foreston, Laney knew she had come around. There were naysayers, of course, but most of the town believed, particularly those who had lived there for a while. And Carmen had seen too much firsthand evidence of magic—from the oddities around the museum to the stories that all-too-frequently emerged from Laney's alterations shop—to deny it any longer. Now she didn't just go along with the legend, she embraced it—as her admonishment to Laney to *keep her temper* had demonstrated.

"Oh, there's a fork missing from the head place setting," Laney commented as her eyes passed over the table.

"That's funny," Carmen said, pushing the chair aside and looking on the floor beneath it. "I know I set it correctly."

As Carmen lifted up the plates and then the charger in case the fork had rolled underneath them, Laney checked the silver box. "You're right, you had to have. There's nothing left in the box." She looked around the dining room, her eyes moving away from the table. Things in this house had a certain *way* of moving in unnatural—or maybe *super*natural was a better word—ways.

To her left, she heard a squeak, a noise that might be mistaken for the chitter of a mouse if you didn't know better. She turned, and a glint in the hallway caught her eye. Sure enough, the fork was lying there on the brightly polished hardwood floor. "Ah, here it is," Laney said, moving toward the silver piece, but then she froze. She could just see it. When she tried to focus on it, it disappeared, but when she turned her head, she could see it in her peripheral vision.

Light.

There was a fae here. Right in front of her. It was poised on the edge of the ornate wooden frame of the painting in front of her. The fork lay directly beneath it. As she approached, she heard the squeak of its voice again, and for about the eleven millionth time in her life, she found herself cursing her poor Sight. Taryn would be able to see the creature with no effort whatsoever. It must have brought the fork here and was watching her, probably laughing at her reaction. Even though brownies and other household elves loved to be helpful, no fae could resist a little bit of mischief. It was just their nature.

Laney crouched to pick up the fork, glancing up at the artwork that the fae had alighted on, hoping to catch a clearer glimpse of the creature. And she did see something, but it wasn't the fae. It was the painting. Was it just her, or did something look different about it?

The painting was an impressionist landscape dating to around 1875, part of the original Paine family's private collection. Rows of tulips in a rainbow of colors stretched out along a meandering creek, with a picturesque windmill in the distance. She straightened, looking the painting over. Something *did* seem different, but she couldn't put her finger on it. Was it just because of the blurry presence of the fae?

Squeak!

"Everything okay?" Carmen called from the dining room.

"Yup," Laney said, turning away from the painting and the chittering glimmer of light. She brought the fork back into the dining room, replacing it beside the charger. "I think we're pretty close to ready inside. I'd better do a quick check of the grounds, though," Laney said. She usually had to check the nature trail daily to ensure there was no litter piling up from visitors. Since the estate was owned by the city, its grounds were a public park and open from dawn to dusk, which meant that there was never a shortage of trash lying around the trails.

"Sounds good. I'll get these boxes put back in the basement," said Carmen.

Laney let herself out through the kitchen door, which was located at the back of the house. There, a formal garden was located, which included a maze of hedgerows lined with beautiful rose bushes in full bloom, and an arbor covered in thick honeysuckle marking the entrance. It was windy today, which made the honeysuckle rustle noisily. Laney gave this garden a quick once-over but found it void of litter. It usually was—whether because of its close proximity to the house or because it was so much more ornate than the rest of the grounds, people seemed to mind their manners here. It was as you got deeper into the woods that visitors tended to turn into slobs, despite the presence of trash cans every hundred feet or so.

As she passed back through the arbor, she paused, admiring the house from this angle. Framed by the honeysuckle, the mansion—with its architectural style marrying popular elements from the Victorian era such as Queen Anne, Second Empire, and Gothic Revival—always looked so charming. *This would be a great angle for the cameraman to film the exterior of the house from,* she thought. But that brought the thought of Paul coming here back to the forefront of her mind, and with it the tumultuous mix of anger, sorrow, embarrassment, and nerves that she'd been grappling with all morning.

She turned away from the house, down the nature trail. She'd look for litter along the way, but the truth was, she needed to go to the warren. She'd feel calmer there. She always did.

Once out of the sunlight and into the shady woods, the temperature seemed to drop about ten degrees—though on a day like today, that wasn't saying much. She made her way down the six rock-cut steps to the lower garden level. Between the trees, she could make out the white canvas of the large pole tent that had been constructed over the tennis court, where the fashion show was going to be held the next afternoon. It was relatively quiet now, apart from the sound of the canvas flapping on the wind; setup wouldn't begin in earnest until tomorrow morning. It would be a mad rush to get everything set up in time for the event, especially with the presence of the news crew. But the museum couldn't afford dedicated security beyond the alarm on the house itself, and with all the valuable items scheduled to be auctioned off, setting up the day before would be impossible.

As Laney strode down the path, the canopy overhead becoming thicker, she caught movement out of the corner of her eye. Rustling in the dry, brown grass that grew alongside the trail. A bird? A squirrel? Or something... else? She smiled to herself as she walked, listening to the sounds of nature around her: the wind whistling through the branches above, the burble of distant water trickling down Blackberry Creek farther up the trail, and the quiet, almost inaudible hum of voices that only a fortunate few could hear.

Finally, a handful of trash in her fists, she emerged into the clearing where the hollow tree stood. A gnarled, knobby Pacific dogwood tree, the only one of its kind that seemed to be growing in the area. It had a thick trunk, particularly for a dogwood; and near the base it was split open, like a tiny doorway, or a parted curtain etched in wood. The top of the tree was bent, with branches only growing out of one side. When you approached it from certain angles, it almost looked like it had no branches at all, as if it were a petrified stump a million years old. While it may not have been *that* ancient, it was certainly older than a dogwood's typical lifespan of eighty years. But the tree wasn't dead. Leaves still grew on its lopsided branches, and every few years, in the spring and sometimes the late summer, it would be covered with brilliant white blossoms.

It was an oddity. Some might say this tree was a freak of nature, somehow managing to survive against the odds, despite how mangled and dead-looking it appeared at first glance. But Laney knew what it really was.

It was magic.

She tossed the trash into the garbage can beside one of the benches where the city had edged the clearing with a delicate bed of native plants. Then she sat, facing the tree, and closed her eyes. She breathed in deeply, trying to let the peacefulness of the clearing soothe her. But even as she did, she heard her own voice in her memory, telling Paul about this enchanted place. Her grandmother had called it a warren—a place where fae congregate, a door to the other world. Laney had thought for sure Paul would scoff when she told him about her town's local legend, but instead he'd smiled and said, *"I'd love to see it. I hope someday you can show it to me."*

Ironic, wasn't it? She could show it to him today if she wanted. But it definitely wouldn't be under the circumstances she'd envisioned five years ago.

"I had a feeling I'd find you here."

Laney opened her eyes with a start to see Taryn standing in front of her, a spark of mischief in her green eyes. Laney sighed. She hadn't heard her sister's approach.

"I saw Crazy Old Bob down on the corner," Taryn said conversationally as she plopped down on the bench beside Laney, not waiting for an invitation. "Think he'll cause a problem for the fashion show?"

Bob was the resident transient of Paine Woods. Technically no one was supposed to enter the park between dusk and dawn, but the museum staff usually looked the other way when it came to Bob. For one thing, unlike the regular tourists, he cleaned up after himself. Once, when she'd come in early for a morning house tour, Laney had seen him in the garden with a hand broom, sweeping all the cobwebs out of the bushes. She'd always had a soft spot for him after that... even if he did have an unsettling way of lurking in the bushes, watching everyone who went by and having conversations with someone who wasn't there.

"He'll be fine. He's harmless," Laney said. "Who's minding the shop?"

"It's noon. I closed it for lunch," said Taryn. "You don't remember your own store's hours? How are you going to manage without me in a week and a half?"

"Whatever," Laney said with a roll of her eyes. Taryn would be heading back to school Labor Day weekend. She was going into her last year of college, finishing her major in business with an emphasis on hospitality management. Taryn's dream for the last ten years had been to open a cozy country inn, ever since their family had taken a vacation to Mendocino, California and stayed at the bed-and-breakfast that had been used as Angela Lansbury's house in *Murder, She Wrote*. Laney had always thought her sister's dedication to such a random career path for so many years was odd; but by the same token, at least Taryn was majoring in something she intended to use, unlike Laney with her English literature degree. Laney was the odd duck in the family, to be honest—their older brother, Matthew, had also gone to college with a career goal in mind, and he'd achieved that. He'd gone to the University of Oregon, gotten a degree in education, and started teaching down there as soon as his practicum was done. It was just Laney who'd had to fall back on her parents' business to support her after graduating without a job prospect to be found.

Although, considering her *talent*, she supposed that was probably for the best in the end. Grams probably would have said it was destiny or something. Laney was dubious as to the existence of destiny, but considering the fact that she had concrete proof that both fae and magic existed, she supposed anything was possible.

"What are you doing here, anyway?" Laney sighed, leaning back against the cool wood of the bench. A gust of wind shook the branches of the dogwood gently.

"Looking for you. You didn't answer my text message."

Laney didn't respond, but she could feel her traitorous face go as red as her hair, which made Taryn start prodding her hard in the side with her finger.

"Ah-ha! See, I was right! That *was* Paul Nelson, wasn't it?"

"Yes," Laney said through gritted teeth.

"I thought so. He was with the camera crew taking footage of all the shops on Main Street this morning," said Taryn, crossing her legs. "But why is he here? That Poppy Gloria person usually does *Around America*, doesn't she?"

"Gloria Shellburg," Laney corrected with a laugh.

Taryn grinned, clearly pleased that she'd managed to erase the scowl from her sister's features. "You know what I think? I think he's here because he wanted to see you."

And the scowl was back. "I sincerely doubt it," Laney replied.

"Well, why not? Maybe he realizes he messed up. Maybe he wants to apologize."

"No," Laney said firmly. "That wouldn't be it." She sighed and added, "Anyway, it was years ago. He's moved on."

Taryn exhaled with frustration. "Are you so sure about that? Because *you* haven't."

"I have so!" Laney protested.

Taryn rolled her eyes. "Come on, Laney. I *know* you. You definitely have not moved on."

Laney didn't respond for a long moment. She just stared at the hollow tree. In the dappled light between the branches and leaves overhead, it almost appeared to sparkle. Just like earlier in the house, Laney thought she saw colors moving, but it was out of focus and blurry, like she was looking through water.

"How's the warren?" she asked, changing the subject away from Paul.

Taryn glanced over at the dogwood tree. "There's a wood sprite watching you."

"Is it laughing?"

Taryn didn't answer, but the way she squirmed, Laney knew the answer was yes.

Finally, Taryn said, "You know how they are. They think

everything we do is funny. We silly humans with our volatile emotions. Don't pay any attention."

Laney nodded sullenly, once again feeling resentful that her sister was able to see the fae so clearly. Their grandma had compared their Sight to regular seeing—Taryn had 20/20 vision, while Laney was in dire need of glasses.

But they didn't make glasses of the magical variety.

Laney had gotten a better deal than poor Matthew, though. He couldn't see fae at all. It had been the cause of dozens of arguments when they were little, and more than one fistfight, truth be told. Their grandma had explained that it was much more common for girls to have the Sight than boys, which Matthew had not found fair at all. And it didn't help matters that Laney and Taryn both had a magical gift that emerged as they grew older, which Grams had called their *faery blessings*. Laney had her "magic touch", of course—she could imbue her will into objects she touched, though it seemed to only occur when she was sewing. Taryn's gift was also one associated with touching objects, though instead of putting something in, she took something out: memories. When Taryn held an antique or something else old, she could sometimes sense the object's past. Both their gifts were volatile, though—they didn't always work. Not everything Taryn held would show her a memory, and not everything Laney stitched would give its wearer good luck or bad luck.

In fact, it seemed like it usually only happened when Laney was *least* hoping it would. Which is why she'd taught herself to only sew when she was in a good mood. She'd learned her lesson from the infamous Band Uniform Incident. She'd been in eighth grade at the time, her brother a sophomore in high school. Matthew, not wanting his parents to know that he'd torn his band uniform pants yet again, had asked her to patch them for him. She'd been in a foul temper because fixing his uniform in time for that evening's football game meant she had to skip watching her favorite TV show with her friend Vanessa. She hadn't expected that Matthew would wind up tripping down the bleacher stairs after the game and breaking his leg. That had been the first in a series of many, many mishaps before Laney had connected the dots and recognized what her faery "blessing" was.

Of course, if she sewed when she was happy, she could bring good fortune to the wearers of her garments, and that was always nice. She supposed her gift was a bit of a mixed bag at the end of the day.

"Do you want me to stay with you for the interview?" Taryn asked. "I could close the shop for the rest of the day."

"No, don't do that. Mrs. Jessop was supposed to come pick up her dress, remember?" Mrs. Jessop lived in The Dalles, not too far west of Foreston but on the south side of the Columbia River, in Oregon. She'd had a tear in her favorite LBD, and it had taken

Laney the better part of two weeks to figure out how to repair the rip in a way that wouldn't be instantly visible (factoring in, of course, breaks to keep herself from getting too frustrated; the last thing she needed was for that frustration to turn into bad luck for Mrs. Jessop the next time she wore the dress). It was close to an hour's drive to get from The Dalles to Foreston, and she'd likely already left.

"Oh, that's right," Taryn said, a note of disappointment in her voice. Laney eyed her. It was just as well. She couldn't completely trust that her sister would be there to be supportive in the way Laney wanted, and not try to stir the pot—which she was sure Taryn would justify as "just trying to help."

But that wasn't the help Laney wanted. Really. She was not interested in getting back with Paul, even if Taryn insisted that she hadn't moved on. After all, the problems—the reasons they'd broken up in the first place—still existed. If anything, they had probably only gotten worse. His fame since his uVer days had only grown.

"Well, hang in there, then," Taryn said, rising from the bench. "Keep me posted. And keep an open mind, okay?"

Laney just rolled her eyes, watching as her sister disappeared down the trail.

With Taryn gone, it was quiet in the clearing. But amid the birdsong and the rustling of leaves in the breeze, she could have sworn she heard laughter, like the tinkling of bells.

Chapter 3

The doorbell rang promptly at one o'clock. Laney had been in the first-floor bathroom, reapplying her lipstick—she wanted to look good on camera, after all—and the sound of the chimes made her freeze in place. She stared at her reflection in the mirror in silent horror for a long moment before Carmen finally appeared over her shoulder.

"You want me to get the door?" Carmen asked, looking at her quizzically.

"No, no," Laney replied, quickly blotting her lips and shutting off the light. Her shoes clopped against the hardwood floor as she made her way to the front door. She breathed in deeply, closing her eyes and whispering a silent prayer that she could do this. Then she opened the door.

No amount of mental preparation could have made her ready

for the moment she saw Paul again. The only consolation she had was that he seemed to be completely taken aback by the sight of her on the other side of the door, which gave her a moment to regain her composure as they both stared at each other, wide-eyed. The photo Taryn had texted her this morning hadn't done him justice. He was even more handsome than she remembered—or maybe it was that he'd grown even more handsome with time. He still wore the gray T-shirt he'd had on in the photo, though now he wore a black blazer over it. Not the best choice in this heat, but it added an air of professionalism and showcased his broad shoulders. His jaw looked a bit more square than it had as a twenty-one-year-old, covered now with rakish stubble. His brown hair, once unruly and downright wild, had been tamed into a neat style that was professional but still just long enough to fit with his slightly nonconformist personality. His skin was more tan, likely from all the time he spent outdoors covering just about every news story you could imagine. Though she'd made a point to avoid the news whenever he was on the screen, sometimes she would catch a glimpse of him on the mounted televisions when she and Carmen would get dinner at the Brownstone Tavern & Grill. She'd seen him everywhere from Florida, reporting on a hurricane's progress as palm branches whipped around behind his head, to the Middle East, discussing the plight of war-torn areas, to Windsor for the most recent royal wedding.

The man in front of her was almost unrecognizable from the boy she'd known five years ago. The only things that remained unchanged were his eyes—the bluest eyes Laney had ever seen. She was still fairly certain she could drown in those eyes.

"Laney," said Paul at last, his voice deep and rich. "This is a surprise. I... was told that I'd be meeting with a woman named Vivian."

Laney swallowed with difficulty. "Viv is out of town. I told her I'd handle it, since I'm in charge of the fashion show." That, of course, had been before she knew who would be conducting the interview, but since Diane had given her no other choice, there was no point splitting hairs.

"Oh. I see. That's right, you used to volunteer at the Foreston museum, didn't you? I suppose it didn't occur to me that that might still be the case." He seemed rattled, which made Laney feel slightly relieved—at least she wouldn't be the only one out of sorts for this interview.

That didn't last long, though. As Laney showed the crew into the house and down to the basement office where they could stow their excess gear, Paul seemed to regain his composure.

"I was hoping to run into you while I was here in town, though," he said, slinging off the duffel bag he'd been carrying over one shoulder.

"Is that so?" Laney asked, keeping her gaze riveted on the

cameraman who came to crouch beside the bag, unzipping it and pulling out a tripod and a few other pieces, the purpose of which Laney could only guess.

"Of course," Paul said earnestly. He sidestepped in front of her so that she couldn't avoid eye contact. "Do you really think I could come here and not want to talk to you?"

Laney stared up at him for a moment, tongue-tied, her face burning. But before she could say anything, someone behind her cleared their throat, and the spell was broken.

"Sorry to interrupt," said a small young woman with vivid purple hair. "Are you the one who's going to be giving the interview?"

"Oh, y-yes, sorry," Laney stammered. "Laney McCarthy. I'm a docent at the museum, and the fashion show coordinator."

"Great. I'm Ashley. Do you have a good place where I can set up shop? I need to get you in makeup while we've still got the light." Ashley held up a small suitcase with her left hand and gestured to it with her right like Vanna White.

Laney blinked. "Makeup?"

Ashley grinned. "You want to look your best on camera!"

"Of course," Laney said, flustered. So much for the extra lipstick she'd thrown on before the crew got here. "Um, how about the bridal room?"

"Right. We can continue our conversation later," Paul said.

"Sure," Laney said, biting her lip. She'd been hoping to avoid continuing the conversation at all, frankly. Ashley looked between the two of them with a dark eyebrow arched, but she said nothing as Laney led her through the office door and down the hall to the bridal room. Though the daylight basement had originally been used by the Paine family for storage, it was still just as elegant as the rest of the house. Leaded windows with diamond-patterned grids provided bright natural light and a charming view of the grounds, perfect for the changing room that had been added by the museum for brides who'd chosen the estate as their wedding venue to get ready for their big day. The rest of the former basement was partitioned into the office Suze used—which doubled as home base for the volunteer docents—and storage for the museum's collections.

It didn't take long for Ashley to do Laney's makeup. Even though it was quite a bit more than Laney herself usually wore, Ashley assured her that it was just enough to make her features pop on camera—a nice, natural look, she promised.

By the time her makeup was done, the rest of the crew had disappeared. Laney showed Ashley up the old servants' staircase from the basement into the kitchen. They followed the sound of voices and found that the camera crew had set up shop in the front parlor, a large stage light pointed at the dress form displaying Laney's Victorian costume. She glanced around the suddenly crowded room; the parlor wasn't exactly small, even for homes of the period; but with the camera crew, light crew, and sound crew together with their equipment, the space was a lot tighter than usual. Paul stood in front of the marble fireplace, talking to Carmen.

"Oh, Laney, there you are," Carmen said when Laney caught her eye. "I suggested they film the interview in here, since we had your dress on display. And the painting, of course." Carmen gestured to the portrait on the wall behind the dress form—another impressionist painting, this one featuring an elegant Victorian woman in a burgundy gown. The painting had served as Laney's inspiration for the costume.

"Good idea," Laney said, coming over to join them.

"Yes, Carmen has been giving me background on this fashion show of yours, Laney," Paul said with a smile. "Sounds like you've done quite well for yourself. McCarthy's Magic Touch?"

"Yeah, well." Laney's face flushed. "A rebrand seemed like a good idea when I took over the shop. The name was my dad's idea, actually." Growing up, her parents' business had just been called *McCarthy's Alterations*. But when they retired and Laney took over, her dad had suggested changing the name to reflect the new ownership and direction for the business. Laney had been mortified at first, but her father had been quick to point out that the costumes Laney had been making and selling on Etsy on the side were a major draw for the shop—particularly because of their reputation for bringing their wearers good luck. In the end, Laney had been unable to deny that, from a marketing standpoint, her dad had a point. "Anyway, should we get this show on the road?"

"All right," said Paul. He gestured to where Laney was to stand while Carmen scooted back to stand with the crew. "We'll open the segment with some establishing shots of Foreston. We took footage downtown this morning, and Monty got some aerial shots with that drone of his." One of the cameramen grinned and gave Laney a sloppy salute. "Voiceover will explain that Foreston is a couple hours northeast of Portland, near The Dalles. Something like, 'Even though Foreston could be pictured in the dictionary next to *sleepy little town*, there are a number of points of interest that make it worth a visit.'"

Laney's eyebrows rose. "Sleepy little town, huh?"

Paul cocked his head. "Would you describe it another way?"

Laney fumbled for a moment. On the one hand, calling it sleepy sounded derogatory. On the other hand, he wasn't exactly wrong...

"Fine, whatever," she said.

Paul smirked, silent laughter forming crinkles around the corner of his eyes. "Then we'll cut to the museum, and then the interview portion. We sent the questions via email last week so you could prepare. Did Vivian pass them on to you?"

Laney nodded. She'd memorized all the questions, spent hours mentally perfecting her answers. But that had been back when she'd been envisioning Gloria Shellburg asking them.

Nothing is different, she reminded herself. *You still know these answers backward and forward.*

"There's no need to be nervous," Paul said. "This isn't live. If you get stuck at any point, we can go back and reshoot it."

"Okay."

"Ready to go?" Paul asked.

Laney nodded again, and then the spotlight aimed at her turned on. She blinked for a moment, dazzled. As her vision reoriented itself, she saw the shadowy silhouette of the cameraman lift his hand, gesturing to Paul. Then Paul launched into his introduction.

"I'm here today with Laney McCarthy, one of the volunteer docents at the Historic Paine Estate Museum. She also just so happens to be the organizer of one of the museum's most popular events, the annual fashion show and auction. Laney, can you tell us a little bit about the event?"

"I, uh..." She stared at the camera aimed in her direction, her mind a blank. All those answers that she'd memorized so well had seemed to flee from her mind the moment that spotlight had turned on. All her brain could focus on was the camera, the lights, all these people, the boom over her head, just out of view of the camera.

"That is…"

"Hey," Paul said softly, nudging her shoulder. "Don't get nervous."

"I'm not nervous," Laney hissed under her breath. "I'm just not used to—that." She waved her hand at the camera crew.

Paul grinned, the crinkles around his eyes appearing again. "Don't worry about *that*. Pretend they're not there. Just look at me. Imagine you're just having a conversation with me, one on one. Like the old days."

Laney's face flushed. *The old days.* Paul always had been so easy for her to talk to. She'd felt like she could tell him anything that went through her mind.

Until the end. You weren't too keen on having an open conversation with him then, a little voice in her head reminded her.

No. She wasn't going to think about that. She had to do this, for the museum. Besides, that was five years ago. She'd moved on. They'd *both* moved on.

She squared her shoulders and nodded. "Okay," she said. "I'm ready. Let's try again."

"That's a girl," Paul said. He turned back into the camera, repeating his introduction and asking again, "Laney, can you tell us a little bit about the event?"

Just talk to Paul, she thought. "Of course," she said aloud. "Well, the Paine Estate was built in 1876, the height of the

Victorian era and near the beginning of the *Belle Époque* in Europe. It was a period of prosperity both in the United States and abroad, the year of the American centennial, and it was a really fascinating period for fashion. And the following decades brought with them so many exciting changes in the fashion world. This event is a celebration of a hundred and fifty years of fashion. We have models showcasing clothing from every era beginning from the time of the house's construction until the modern day. After the show is over, most of the items worn by the models are available to bid on in our silent auction."

"So if you think bustles are the height of fashion, you're in luck?" Paul joked.

"Some of our re-creations from 1870s and 1880s women's fashion do include bustles, yes," Laney laughed. "But if you're looking for something a little more contemporary, we have a number of designers and high-end boutiques from Portland who have donated both full outfits and individual items like tops, pants, skirts, and so on to the auction."

"And I understand that many of the period costumes were made by you personally, is that right?"

"Yes," Laney said. "I own an alterations shop in town, but I do also sew period-accurate costumes on the side. I've sold them through my Etsy shop for several years now, so making some to donate to the auction seemed like a great way to have a little bit of fun and support the museum at the same time."

"And the word on the street is that your costumes can fetch even more than one of those Portland designers' ensembles. I was speaking to one of the other docents earlier and she told me about your so-called 'magic touch.' Rumor has it that wearing an outfit you've worked on can bring good luck. Would you care to comment?"

Laney shot a panicked glare over at Carmen, who shrugged helplessly. "That wasn't one of the questions from the email," she said, turning back to Paul.

"I know. I thought it might be fun to include a little bit about the magic of Foreston in the segment," Paul said.

Laney's face burned. "No one's going to believe that," she whispered tersely.

"I do," Paul protested.

"They're going to think we're a bunch of superstitious backwoodsmen out here!"

"I don't." Paul looked at her earnestly.

He held her eyes for a long moment, until, to her own surprise, she heard herself saying, "Fine. But it's really silly, honestly."

Paul didn't drop his gaze. "We want to hear about it."

Laney sighed. "People have said things they've bought from me have brought them good luck. I have a tendency to talk to myself when I sew, kind of... imagining what might happen to the things I make when they become someone else's. People noticed that some of those things have come true."

"Such as?"

Laney shifted uncomfortably. "Well, usually it's small stuff, like... they meet their future husbands while wearing one of my dresses, or something. But this one time, I made a bodice. You know, one of those ones women wear over blouses at Renaissance Faires? It was black with red trim, and I thought it looked sort of like a pirate's. So while I was working on it, I said, 'You're destined for an adventure, I think.' A woman bought it from me to wear to Highland Fest. That's a Scottish Games festival down in central Oregon. Apparently on her way there her car broke down on an old logging road and she had no cell reception. She had to leave her car and wander through the forest for two days until she could find help. She wound up using a mirror from her makeup kit to attract the attention of a forestry helicopter that was passing over. They sent a ranger to check and found her there, cold and hungry but otherwise fine."

"Wow," said Paul. "I'd say that definitely counts as an adventure."

"Yeah, I suppose," Laney said, running a hand through her hair. "Afterward she swore the bodice gave her good luck. She said what were the odds that a helicopter would ever see something so small? I don't know if you can count that as good luck, if you believe that what I said to the bodice sent her on that adventure to begin with, but"—she shrugged—"that's what they all say now."

"You've got me convinced," Paul said, and, to Laney's surprise, he sounded genuine. "So, what kind of adventure could a person expect if they were to buy this outfit, for example?" He gestured to the burgundy costume on the dress form beside them.

"Oh, I was careful when I sewed this one," Laney said with a laugh. "Just general good thoughts."

"Can you tell us a little about this costume?"

"Sure. This is a replica Victorian. Usually when I make a costume, I just go for general period accuracy in terms of materials, silhouette, and so on. But this one is actually based on a real outfit, or at least an artist's impression of an outfit from the time." She pointed to the portrait on the wall behind the dress form.

"Oh, yes, I see the resemblance," Paul said, looking from the real dress in front of him to the painting.

"This painting by impressionist artist Enzo Faucheux dates to around the time of the house's construction, and it was part of the original owners' private collection—" She broke off abruptly. There it was again. Another glimmer, another blur of color. A fae, perched on the portrait's ornate wooden frame. She would have thought nothing of it—just assumed that the fae was watching the crowd of newcomers with curiosity and amusement—were it not for what she noticed at the same time.

There was something different about this painting. And this time, she knew exactly what it was.

She looked back at Paul, hoping panic wasn't written on her face. But clearly something was, because Paul's brows furrowed with concern.

He opened his mouth as if to say something, but he was interrupted by the sound of Diane storming down the hall, her high heels clicking noisily on the hardwood floor. The older woman was already an imposing five-foot-eleven as it was, but she routinely wore heels, as if to make herself even more intimidating. "Are you about done?" she demanded, coming into the parlor. "I've got important phone calls to make, and I can't hear myself think over all the noise you're making."

"Diane, we're filming the interview," Carmen protested.

"Really? From what I could hear, it sounds like you're filming a commercial for McCarthy's Magic Touch," Diane snapped.

"We're terribly sorry, ma'am," Paul said. "I think we're about done in here. If we could just get some footage of the rest of the museum...?"

Diane rolled her eyes. "If you must. But *please* be *quiet*. Some of us have real work to do around here."

She stormed back down the hall, her heels clip-clopping in a way that reminded Laney uncannily of a horse. The office door slammed behind her.

"Wow," Paul said when she was gone.

"Wow, indeed," Laney agreed.

"Is she always like that?"

Laney nodded, rolling her eyes. "She used to have her office down in the basement where the collections manager's office is, but she complained so much about the noise from the volunteers in the basement that she managed to worm her way upstairs. Now she shares Viv's office." She lowered her voice and added. "I think she really wanted a better opportunity to snoop on the museum goings-on than she could get downstairs. In case you can't tell, she's the queen of the busybodies."

"That much is obvious," Paul agreed.

"So, where else would you like us to film in the museum?" Monty the cameraman asked Laney.

Laney hesitated a moment, her mind still whirling from Diane's interruption and the discovery she'd made just before. She glanced back at the painting. The glimmer of light was gone, but the painting was still definitely different.

Paul glanced at Laney sidelong for a moment before turning to Carmen. "Ms. Rocha, you did a great job suggesting our first filming location," he said. "Would you be so kind as to give the crew a tour? I've got a few more questions for Ms. McCarthy—off-the-record."

Carmen grinned, giving Laney a sly look. Laney was too

preoccupied with her own thoughts even to protest. "Of course," Carmen said. "Right this way."

When the crew had gone, Paul turned back to Laney. "All right, what's up?"

"Up?" Laney repeated.

"I saw that look you got when you were talking about the painting. Is something wrong?"

Laney glanced over her shoulder to the doorway to the hall. Diane's door was shut, but still... She tiptoed over and, as quietly as she could, pulled the door to the room closed. Then she crept back over to the portrait, looking at it carefully once more. "This isn't the real painting."

"What?"

"It's a good imitation. *Really* good. I probably wouldn't have realized anything was wrong if I hadn't spent so much time staring at it when I made this dress. But look at this." She pulled her phone out, flipping through her photos until she found a shot she'd taken of the painting so she wouldn't have to remove it from the house while working on the costume. "Here in the lower right corner. There's a tear, do you see? It's been that way as long as I've worked here. But look." She pointed to the painting hanging on the wall now.

"There's no tear in that canvas," Paul said slowly.

"Exactly," Laney said. Her stomach turned over

uncomfortably, as if Paul's confirmation somehow made it real.

"So this one is a forgery?"

"It must be." Laney bit her lip. "And that's not all," she said, remembering the landscape in the hallway outside the dining room. It was another Faucheux, and it had looked different to her this morning as well, but she hadn't been able to put her finger on it. Was that one a forgery, too?

"This morning—" she began, but a thud above her head made her jump.

Paul looked up at the ceiling. "I should probably go check on my crew and make sure they're not demolishing your museum. Can we continue this discussion later? Maybe over dinner?"

Laney hesitated as he caught her green eyes with his blue ones, and her heart flip-flopped involuntarily. It had been five years— how did he still have this pull over her?

She should tell him no. She should tell him never mind. She should tell him to just forget it and figure this out on her own. She'd broken up with him for a reason, after all. *Remember the pub. Remember what happened that night,* she warned herself.

But to her own consternation, she heard herself answering, "Yeah. That would be good."

Chapter 4

Laney sat sullenly at the bar of the Brownstone Tavern & Grill. In her nervousness, she'd already pulled the label off her bottle of cider, folded it into a teeny tiny pie slice, unfolded it again, and then shredded it to pieces with her fingernails. She hadn't touched the drink itself; her stomach was full of too many butterflies. Why had she agreed to meet him here? Her mind played out a dozen different scenarios as to how this evening could go, and none of them were good.

Of course, the reason she'd agreed was obvious. Those blue eyes of his left her tongue-tied. Even back during that year when they'd dated, sometimes he'd give her that look, his eyes sparkling with mischief, and she'd find herself unable to speak. She'd built up a bit of immunity to it the longer they'd been together, but now that they'd been apart for five years, all that immunity was gone. If he'd asked her to meet him on the moon, she'd have tracked down the nearest NASA facility and found a way to commission a rocket. Paul Nelson was dangerous to her health, and she should leave now while she still could.

Then again... she needed to talk to someone about the paintings. She didn't feel comfortable calling the police herself until Suze or Viv got back. After all, what if she was mistaken? Maybe the museum had had the tear in the canvas repaired and had neglected to mention it to her. And maybe she was wrong about the landscape being different; maybe that had been her imagination. Maybe she was making something out of nothing.

But her gut told her otherwise. Something was definitely wrong here. The fae had been trying to alert her to something. And Paul wanted to help her, so she should accept his help. Right?

She inhaled, looking down at the droplets of condensation the bottle left on the cardboard coaster. It would be fine as long as they kept the discussion focused on the paintings. There was no need to talk about what had happened between them. Especially that night five years ago, the week before Laney was due to return to the States. They were going out to the corner pub with a group of friends from the university, and some of Paul's old schoolmates that he was eager for her to meet before she went back. Normally they would have headed over to the pub together, but that night she'd been working late on getting some costume repairs done for the theatre department. She'd promised to do it a few weeks before, but finishing up her end-of-term papers had taken up too much time. But now that those were done, she hadn't wanted to go back on her word.

She'd cheerfully finished up the patching and the hemming and the button replacements, returning the last costume to its garment bag and hanging it on its rack. Then she'd headed over to the pub, but when she got there...

Her face grew hot now as she remembered seeing that other woman's arms around Paul's neck, and she clenched her teeth.

The door opened behind Laney as a new group of patrons entered the restaurant, bringing with them a gust of wind and, on it, the strong scent of wood smoke. She'd noticed the smell earlier as she walked from her apartment to the Brownstone, but it seemed to be stronger now. She wondered if someone nearby had a fire pit. The fire marshal had put out a warning last month that outdoor burning was prohibited, but when had that ever stopped anyone?

"Hey," said a voice in her ear, and Laney jumped, nearly falling off her barstool. Her heart pounding in her ears, she turned to face a chagrined Carmen. "Sorry," Carmen apologized. "He's not here yet?"

"No. What are you doing here?"

"What, I'm not allowed to get dinner with my sister at my favorite restaurant?" Carmen looked pointedly over her shoulder to where her sister Claudia was standing at the host's podium waiting for someone to seat them. Claudia had recently gone through a messy divorce and was staying with Carmen and Josh while she figured out her future living arrangements. Since Josh frequently traveled out of the country for work, Carmen was glad to have her sister around for company during the times when he was gone. Such as right now—Josh was currently in the UAE for the next two weeks.

Laney quirked an eyebrow at her. "The timing seems a little suspicious."

Carmen made a face of mock offense. "There's nothing suspicious about it! You know I don't have a snoopish bone in my body. Them, on the other hand..." She gestured to a table just outside the bar area. Laney looked just in time to see Taryn's blonde head duck down behind the wood-paneled half-wall separating the bar area from the rest of the restaurant.

Laney's eyes widened and she hopped off her high bar stool, leaving her drink and Carmen in the dust as she stormed over to the table. "Seriously?" she demanded, finding her parents sitting across from Taryn at the small, square table.

"Oh, hello, dear," her mother, Nancy, said cheerfully. "We didn't realize you were here!"

"Nice try, Mom," Laney said with a roll of her eyes. "What do you think you're doing here?"

"We're just getting dinner," Taryn said innocently. "What, is that a crime now?"

"Aren't you supposed to be at work?" Laney asked her sister.

"Shift doesn't start until eight," Taryn replied. In addition to filling in at the alterations shop during the day, Taryn worked evenings at the Penngrove Hotel—sometimes as a hostess in the restaurant, sometimes working the night desk. Laney usually felt a bit guilty that she kept her sister's days tied up at the shop; Taryn would probably have better hours at the hotel if it weren't for her. The hotel management knew Taryn was one of their best workers. Tonight, however, Laney couldn't manage to find any sympathy.

"And you just coincidentally happened to choose to come to dinner at the Brownstone tonight."

"Well, of course. You know it's our favorite—" Nancy began.

Laney shot a glare at her mom, and her father, Aden, nudged his wife with his elbow. "I think you better drop it, honey," he murmured. "She's not buying it."

"You've never been a good liar, Mom," Taryn said, shaking her head.

Nancy sighed. "I just wanted to see him in person! We never got a chance to meet him when you were in England, and now I see him on the TV all the time and he just looks so *handsome*—"

"Mother!" Laney snapped, glancing over her shoulder to make sure Paul hadn't come into the restaurant yet to hear this mortifying exchange. "Do you *mind*? How did you find out that I was meeting Paul here, anyway? I deliberately didn't tell a certain *someone*."

She narrowed her eyes at her sister.

"Well, another certain *someone* may have let it slip," Taryn retorted, looking past Laney's shoulder. Laney turned to see Carmen approaching the table, Claudia following behind.

"Thanks a lot, blabbermouth," Carmen said sarcastically to Taryn.

"Great. Glad to know that I can trust no one in this town," Laney cried in exasperation.

"Sorry," Carmen said, looking chagrined. "I only found out about all this today, and when Laney said she was meeting him for dinner, I just got curious."

"So what *is* going on here, anyway?" Claudia asked, nudging her way between Laney and Carmen. "Laney and Paul Nelson used to be a couple?"

"Yes," Laney said through gritted teeth.

"Why'd you break up? I've seen him on the news and he is a *hottie*." Claudia mimed fanning herself, making Laney's face grow even redder.

"She won't tell anyone!" Taryn exclaimed. "I've been trying to find out for years and she keeps giving me nonsense answers like, '*I realized we wouldn't work out long-term.*' Whatever that means."

"That's not a nonsense answer, it's the truth!" Laney protested. "And, as I've said *repeatedly* over the years, I don't want to talk about it!" She looked around again to make sure that Paul hadn't come in. That would be the only way this day could get worse, if

Paul overheard this conversation.

"Okay, guys, I think we need to cool it," Aden broke in then, giving his older daughter a look of concern. "We're making Laney upset. Maybe we ought to just get our food to go."

"I think that sounds like a *fantastic* idea—" Laney began, but the buzzing of her phone in her back pocket made her jump. She pulled out her phone to read the text message that had just come in. It was from an unknown number with a New York area code.

I'm so sorry, I won't be able to make it tonight. The network wants me to cover the fire. Stay safe. -P

Laney reread the message in confusion. This had to be from Paul. He was canceling on her? She knew she should be relieved, but irrationally, her heart sank.

She reread the message again. What did he mean by *the fire?*

She looked up at the crowd around the table, her brows furrowed. "Did you guys hear anything about—"

As she spoke, one of the other restaurant patrons called out behind her, "Hey, wait, turn that up! That's by my house!"

Laney glanced up as the bartender turned the volume up on one of the wall-mounted TVs that had been playing the local news on mute. She started as she saw one of the Channel 7 field reporters standing on the shoulder of what looked like Highway 14. Behind him, the forest glowed a deep, ominous orange. A red banner on the bottom of the screen read *WILDFIRE IN THE COLUMBIA RIVER GORGE.*

As the volume on the television increased, Laney heard the reporter saying, *"Though it's believed to have only been burning for three hours, with high winds, higher temperatures, and inflammable forest undergrowth due to an unusually dry summer, the front of this fire has already managed to spread ten miles in a northeasterly direction, heading rapidly in the direction of the communities of Fernhill and Foreston."*

Laney gasped as the voices of the other restaurant patrons around her rose in alarm. She strained to hear the rest of the reporter's words over the cacophony.

"The blaze is believed to have been sparked by an improperly extinguished campfire at a state park near the Oregon-Washington border. Southwestern Washington has been under a no-burn ordinance for over a month due to high fire risk. Fernhill and Foreston residents are urged to have an evacuation plan in place and to be ready to leave at a moment's notice should the local officials deem an evacuation necessary."

Laney turned away from the television to her family, who sat around the table in silent shock. She swallowed, suddenly overwhelmed by the sensation that she was standing on the brink of a steep cliff with nothing to hold on to for balance.

She'd thought her day couldn't get any worse.

How wrong she'd been.

Chapter 5

The evening passed in a panicked blur. As the gravity of the news report hit them, restaurant patrons had rushed out of the Brownstone to get back to their homes and pack in case of an evacuation—Laney's parents and Carmen and Claudia among them. Though the fire was still quite a ways off, the authorities warned that homes southwest of Foreston were most at risk. The McCarthy family home fit that description, but Carmen's house was even farther out of town, in Fernhill, an unincorporated community southwest of Foreston, deeper in the national forest.

Taryn had wanted to go back to the house with their parents, but they'd been insistent she stay in town and keep her shift at the Penngrove. "We don't actually know that the fire will make it as far as town, or even as far as our house," Aden had reasoned. "The winds might die down or change direction. There's no sense in panicking."

Still, it had been hard for Laney to do anything *but* panic. The bartender had changed the channel on all the other televisions away from sports and onto various different news stations, and the remaining patrons in the restaurant sat quietly watching. The volume was only turned up on the local station, Channel 7, but all the national cable news networks were covering the fire as well. Laney tried to keep her eyes focused on the Channel 7 screen, but she found her eyes kept wandering over to the TV to the right. The newsroom anchors kept cutting to the reporter live on the scene, Paul Nelson. He was still dressed in his gray tee and black blazer from earlier, but Laney couldn't help but notice that the sparkle she'd seen in his blue eyes earlier in the day had faded. Now his face was grim, and as the sky grew darker, the orange glow above the trees burned ever brighter.

When it was time for Taryn to head to work, Laney had returned to her apartment over the store. By now, the smoky smell had grown so strong that she wondered how she ever could have mistaken it for a fire pit. It was only a short walk back, but by the time she made it into the store and shut the door, she was coughing and her lungs itched and burned.

When her parents had owned the store, they'd used the apartment above the shop for storage, but when Laney had taken over the business, she'd converted it back into an apartment and updated it. She'd still been living at home up until that point and had relished the opportunity for some independence, but now she found herself wishing that she'd gone back home with her parents tonight, even if they had insisted on not panicking just yet. She was worried about their home, about their dog, a senior golden retriever named Bailey, and about her parents themselves. What if the fire spread quickly and they weren't able to evacuate in time? She was sure the sheriff wouldn't let that happen; the fire was still more than twenty miles away, so they had plenty of lead time. But even if they evacuated in time, they were both in their sixties, and while they were both in good health, she knew that the danger of complications from smoke inhalation increased the older you got.

As she unlocked the door at the top of the stairs and let herself into her apartment, her phone—ordinarily on vibrate only—let out a shrill set of beeps. Her heart raced erratically as she came into the apartment, tossing her keys and small clutch onto the table beside her door, then yanked her phone out of her back pocket. It was an automated message that must have gone out to every cell phone in the region: *Emergency alert—prepare for action. The communities of* FERNHILL, WASHINGTON *and* FORESTON, WASHINGTON *should be ready to evacuate at a moment's notice.*

She swallowed as she stared down at the screen, reading it over and over again. That message was like a freezing bucket of ice water dumped right over her head. This was real. This was happening.

Foreston was never going to be the same again, was it?

Her phone buzzed in her hand, and she jumped, but it wasn't another emergency alert. It was a text message. Multiple text messages, in fact—several had flooded in at once.

The first was from Taryn: *Did that give anyone besides me a heart attack?*

Then Carmen: *Got back to the house just in time. The sheriff told us to pack a bag and be ready to leave at any time.*

Matthew: *I just saw the news, are you ok? Are mom and dad ok???*

Her mom: *No evacuation notice for us yet. I've got Bailey's things packed and am working on ours. I'm getting things together for Taryn, too, in case she doesn't get back from work in time.*

Her dad: *Is there any way to turn off those emergency alerts? They're loud enough to wake the dead!*

In spite of everything, Laney felt her lips twitch into a small smile at that last one. *No, dad,* she tapped out with her thumb. *You need to leave them on in case they send an evacuation notice or road closure information or something.* She pressed send on that and then turned her attention to the other ones. She had just finished telling Matthew that everyone was okay and that their parents were getting ready to evacuate when more messages started pouring in.

Suze: *I got the alert and I'm on my way back now.*

Dina, one of the designers who had donated to the fashion show: *What's going to happen with the event tomorrow? I heard they're closing Highway 14.*

Viv: *What's going on up there? A fire?! Do you need me to get off at the next port of call?*

And that New York number again: *How are you holding up?*

Laney swallowed, her eyes lingering on the last message. Then she swiped it aside and opened her phone's browser, searching for the sheriff's informational number. She dialed it, listened to the whole message, and then sighed as she ended the call. There was no time to dwell on Paul's texts or on her worry for her parents or anything else now. She had a *lot* of phone calls to make.

Laney hardly slept that night. Her call to the sheriff's information line had verified that, indeed, all roads into Foreston were closed except to emergency personnel and residents. And even if they tried to proceed with the event without any out-of-town vendors or guests, bringing that many people to the museum when there was a possible evacuation looming over their heads—not to mention holding an outdoor event with so much smoke in the air—would be an obvious disaster. The fashion show would have to be canceled, and with just eighteen hours until it was supposed to start, Laney would have to work fast.

By the time she got done calling all the vendors to let them know the event had been postponed indefinitely, it was almost midnight. From there she moved to her computer, updating the museum's website and social media to notify visitors of the cancellation; emailing everyone who had purchased advance tickets online; and sending out the museum's newsletter to hopefully catch anyone who had been planning to buy tickets at the door and may have missed the other notices. She'd still have to call everyone who'd purchased tickets in person or over the phone—mostly older people who didn't use computers as much—but that would have to be done in the morning.

While she worked, she had the TV in her small living room turned to the news. She knew the smart thing would have been to stick with Channel 7, but for some reason she found herself surfing until she landed on the national news.

"Paul Nelson is live on the scene..."

Even as she sent emails and posted updates late into the night, her mind kept wandering back to one thing. And as she lay in bed, well after three A.M., in between worries about the fire and her family and Carmen and the museum and the fashion show and everything else, the thought continued to pop into her head, keeping her awake until the sky overhead was starting to brighten with dawn.

She hadn't given Paul her phone number yesterday. But she still had the same number she'd had in college.

After all these years—even after a move overseas and changing his own—Paul had saved her number.

Chapter 6

The next morning at eight o'clock, Laney trudged blearily from the museum's parking lot across the small grassy area toward the house. She felt sicker after sleeping a few hours than she probably would have if she hadn't slept at all.

The air quality wasn't helping matters. Overnight the smoke had accumulated beyond just the bad smell—now it was thick in the air like fog, making the morning sun glow an eerie orange. She could barely draw a breath and had to pull the collar of her shirt up over her nose and mouth to try to filter some of it out. She'd seen people on social media recommending everyone get N95 respirators to wear outdoors. Supposedly Friedman's, the hardware store across the street from the alterations shop, had some in stock, so Laney was planning on stopping there once she was done making all the phone calls she needed to today. They didn't open until nine, so she'd been unable to get any before she left for the museum.

As she reached the foot of the stairs into the house, she heard a noise to her right. The gardens had been quieter than usual today, as if most of the birds had fled the smoke, and the squirrels were keeping close to their dens. But she'd heard a few stubborn chirps and squeaks from the parking lot, and now, among them, a voice. Deep and gravelly, a low murmur.

She came around the side of the house, looking into the rhododendrons that grew next to it, the sticky remains of their spent blossoms from this spring still present among the leaves. Sure enough, crouching in the bushes in the shade of a large yew was Bob, having a conversation with someone who definitely wasn't there.

When he heard Laney approach, he glanced over the shoulder of his thin brown coat but didn't stand up. He kept right on muttering to himself.

"Hey, Bob," Laney said as she drew near. "Are you doing okay in all this smoke?"

"About as well as any other wild thing," Bob grumbled. He looked down at the empty space at his feet once more, then finally straightened—though "straight" for Bob still involved a rather significant hunch.

"Have you been able to keep up with the news? I don't know

if you have a radio or cell phone..." Laney trailed off expectantly, but Bob just grunted. "I just want to make sure you know if evacuation orders come through," Laney went on. "Do you have a place to evacuate to?"

"I'm not evacuating," Bob said, waving his hand dismissively.

Laney struggled for a moment to resist gritting her teeth in frustration. "Bob, I know it's difficult, but if the sheriff says we need to evacuate, we have to follow his orders. It's for your own safety. During a wildfire, Paine Woods is one of the most dangerous places you could be."

"That's why I'm not evacuating," Bob reiterated. "Someone has to look after this place and the creatures living in it. I can see that you're not going to."

Laney's temper flared in spite of herself. "I'm *trying* to look after *one* of them," she retorted. Bob simply harrumphed in reply.

She rolled her eyes and turned away. It was obvious she wasn't going to get anywhere with Crazy Old Bob. He wasn't going to take care of himself, which meant *she'd* have yet another thing she'd have to take care of. She made a mental note to grab a case of water and an extra pack of respirators at Friedman's later.

"Your sister's down at the hollow tree," Bob called after her.

Laney halted in her tracks. "What?" she snapped. "What's she doing there?"

Bob gave her a beady-eyed stare. "Why don't you tell me?"

Laney rolled her eyes. "I guess I'll go find out," she muttered, turning back down the path around the house and into the woods. She was so furious, she didn't even notice the glimmers of light in the trees overhead, watching her.

Behind her, a lone bird chirped noisily until she got too far away to hear.

By the time she emerged into the clearing, Laney was panting and her chest hurt. "What are you doing here?" she demanded, seeing her sister sitting cross-legged on the ground at the foot of the dogwood tree.

Taryn turned her head, and Laney saw she was wearing a mask. "You said you weren't going to open the store today," Taryn said, rummaging through the leather backpack on the ground beside her, pulling out another respirator from a Ziploc bag and handing it to Laney. "We had some of those in the supply closet at the hotel."

"The store being closed doesn't have anything to do with the question I just asked you," Laney said.

Taryn ignored her. "Mold the metal clip over your nose," she said.

"I know," Laney replied tersely, fitting the mask over her face. She didn't notice an obvious difference, but she was sure this was better for her than walking around with her face shoved into her shirt collar. What would be even *better*, of course, would be for them to go inside, out of the smoke. She told Taryn as much.

Taryn uncrossed her legs and looked down at her scuffed plaid All Stars. "I needed to check on the warren," she finally said. "Make sure the fae were okay. The other wildlife seem to be fleeing in advance of the fire, but the fae..." She furrowed her brows, looking back at the hollow tree. "I don't think they can. Or if they do, I don't think they'll come back."

Laney felt herself go cold, ice shooting through her veins. "Are you sure? I mean, how can you know that? It's not like the fae can actually tell you, right?" Laney had to struggle to hear fae voices clearly—usually to her they just sounded like some weird kind of bird or squirrel—but when she had heard them, they'd sounded like they were speaking gibberish. Even Taryn had said she'd never really been able to understand what they were saying.

"I don't know," Taryn admitted. "It's just... a *feeling* I'm getting. Like they're telling me without words."

Laney's stomach knotted as she stood beside her sister, looking up at the tree. *Why can't I see you better?* she thought in frustration. *Why do you favor Taryn over me? I love you just as much, don't I?*

"So what can we do?" she asked aloud.

"I don't know," Taryn said. "Just pray, I guess. Pray that the firefighters can get the wildfire out before it reaches Foreston. Or that even if it does make it up here, that it somehow misses the Paine Estate."

Laney nodded. Her eyes were burning, only partially from the smoke. "We should get inside," she said, her voice rough.

"Yeah," Taryn agreed, getting to her feet.

"You headed back home?" Laney asked.

Taryn nodded. "Mom said she packed an emergency bag for me, but who knows whether she put the right stuff in it or not."

"Do you think you're going to have to evacuate?"

Taryn shrugged. "I hope not. Matthew wants Mom and Dad to come stay with him in Eugene, though. Even if we don't have to evacuate the house. He's worried about the smoke on their lungs."

"That was bothering me, too," Laney said. "Do you think they'll do it?"

"Doubtful. I don't think they want to leave the house unless they absolutely have to. And they won't want to leave us here, either."

"You wouldn't go with them?" Laney asked.

Taryn gave her a look. "I've got work," she said.

"I'm sure the hotel wouldn't mind. You're leaving in a week anyway, to go back to school."

Taryn shook her head. "Things are crazy. Most of Fernhill got evacuated, so a bunch of the evacuees are staying at the Penngrove now. We filled up overnight. I can't just leave them now."

Laney frowned. Carmen's house was in Fernhill. Had she and Claudia gotten evacuated? Josh was overseas right now for his job. He was probably in a state of panic.

"What about you?" Taryn asked. "Are you going to evacuate?"

"I can't. Not until the sheriff makes me," Laney said. "I have to look after the store, and the museum, and..." She trailed off, glancing back at the hollow tree. If Taryn was right, and the fae couldn't leave...

"Yeah," Taryn said quietly. "We're on the same page there."

Laney nodded, and the sisters walked silently back toward the house.

Chapter 7

Laney walked Taryn to her car, then headed back to the museum. She'd taken an extra mask from Taryn to give to Bob, but by the time she made it back to the house, the old man was nowhere to be seen. Laney sighed, then coughed. He was not making this easy for her.

As she entered the house, she heard voices coming from Viv's office. She winced, stopping in the foyer to catch her breath, inhaling the clean indoor air deeply. Diane was already here. Laney had kind of hoped that she could make all her phone calls and head out before she got here. No such luck.

She steeled herself, then walked down the hall to the office. The door was open, and Laney saw that Suze was inside, leaning against Viv's empty desk. She looked just as exhausted as Laney did.

"There you are," Diane said, looking up as Laney came in the door. "The phone has been ringing off the hook. People want to know if the fashion show is canceled."

"I said it would have to be," Suze said in a gentler voice. "They were already closing Highway 14 when I drove home last night. Inbound traffic is for residents only."

"Well, anyone with common sense would know that," Diane snipped. "I just said it wasn't my place to make that call."

Laney gritted her teeth. "Yes, the fashion show is canceled," she said. The smug look that washed over Diane's face told her that she had only asked the question just to hear Laney give that answer. *Bitter old prune*, Laney thought, trying to get her temper in line. "I emailed all the vendors and ticket-holders last night, and I updated the website. I'm also going to be calling everyone this morning."

"Let me know if you need help with that," Suze offered.

"Thanks, that would be a big help," Laney said. "How was your conference?"

"It was fine. But I would have stayed here if I'd known what was going to happen. How did the interview go yesterday?"

"Yes, Laney," Diane said, her brow arched. "How did it go? From what I overheard, it sounded like your renewed acquaintance with Paul Nelson did not, in fact, cause you to spontaneously combust as you'd feared."

Suze blinked in confusion. "Paul Nelson? You know Paul

Nelson, Laney?"

Mercifully, Laney was spared having to answer that question by the phone ringing. She snatched the phone off Viv's desk before either Diane or Suze could react. "Paine Estate Museum. This is she. Yes, Mrs. Grumbacher, the fashion show is canceled. No, we haven't rescheduled it yet. Yes, we will be refunding the tickets ASAP."

When she hung up, Suze stood. "We should go downstairs and start making those phone calls," she said.

Laney nodded and followed Suze out of the office. But as they started down the hallway, a glimmer of light caught her peripheral vision, and she froze in her tracks. A fae was trying to get her attention again—poised on the same painting she'd noticed yesterday. How could she have forgotten? The fire had driven it out of her mind entirely.

"Suze," Laney said in a low voice, gesturing her over to the painting. The light seemed to flicker frantically for a moment, then disappeared as Suze approached. "I forgot to tell you—I noticed this yesterday. Does this painting look different to you?"

Suze was quiet for a moment, her expression unreadable as she looked at the artwork. "I don't see anything different about it," she said at last.

Laney's heart sank. Had she been wrong? Suze was the collections manager—if the painting had been swapped as she and

Paul had theorized yesterday, wouldn't Suze notice it? Did it really only look different to her because of the fae on the frame? But why would the fae have been trying to get her attention to begin with—and again, just now—if it didn't want her to see something about it?

"Okay, come and look at this one," she urged, pulling Suze into the parlor, where the Victorian lady's portrait still hung behind the replica costume. She felt almost frantic as Suze looked it over. "Do you see? The tear in the corner is missing."

Suze sucked in a breath. "You're right," she said.

Laney let out a sigh of relief. So she wasn't wrong. "I'm assuming the museum didn't get this painting repaired, right?"

"No, it didn't," Suze said.

"Then this painting is a forgery," said Laney.

Suze nodded. "It's a great copy. Almost flawless. How did you notice the difference?"

Laney hesitated. Suze had only lived in Foreston for about as long as Carmen, and unlike Carmen, Suze had never really bought into the town legends of the fae. "I spent a lot of time with this one while I was working on that replica," she finally said, gesturing to the dress on the mannequin.

Suze nodded again, thinking silently for a moment. "Did you call the sheriff?"

"No, I wanted to check with you first and make sure I wasn't wrong."

Suze sighed. "We'd better tell Diane."

"Well, we can't call the sheriff now," were the first words out of Diane's mouth when Laney told her what she'd discovered.

Laney blinked, unsure that she'd heard correctly. "Excuse me?"

Diane rolled her eyes. "Do you or do you not recall that the entire county is currently on fire? The sheriff has more important things to be dealing with right now."

Laney's mouth opened and closed several times, but no words came out. At last, she snapped, "Diane, at least two very expensive paintings have been stolen, and you think that we shouldn't call the sheriff?"

"No, I think we *should* have called the sheriff—*yesterday*, when you noticed that the paintings had been altered. It's astounding to me that apparently interacting with an ex-beau is more momentous to you than the largest fire in this region's recent history, but apparently your priorities must be warped."

"Diane, that's not fair," Suze said, but she shot Laney a sideways glance, her eyebrows high on her forehead, and Laney's face burned with embarrassment. "She wanted to confirm with me, as the museum's collections manager, that the paintings actually had been swapped before acting unilaterally."

Diane huffed. "Well, then, Ms. Collections Manager. What do *you* think we should do?"

Suze hesitated a moment, then sighed. "We need to call the sheriff. Surely they can spare one deputy to just make a report. And even if they tell us we have to wait, at least we'll have notified them. We'll need to have that paper trail if the museum has to make a claim with our insurance provider."

Diane rolled her eyes. "Fine, then. Call the sheriff. See what he tells you. Now if you'll excuse me, I have a lot of work to do. You're not the only one who's affected by this fire, you know," she said sourly to Laney. "I've got brides calling me in a panic about whether their weddings can continue. So you go make your phone calls and I'll make mine."

She shooed Laney and Suze out of her office and slammed the door behind them.

"She's in a great mood this morning," Laney muttered under her breath as they headed for the stairs to the basement.

"She's just stressed," Suze said, her tone unconvincing.

Laney glanced over her shoulder to make sure they were out of earshot of the office before asking in a low voice, "Did you think it was weird that she didn't want us to call the sheriff?"

Suze frowned, pausing as she opened the door to the stairs. "Well... I mean, she is stressed. And she does like to contradict you, usually for no good reason," she pointed out.

"True," Laney agreed, following Suze down to the office. But still, she couldn't help but think...

Someone had to have swapped those paintings.

Chapter 8

The wait on the sheriff's non-emergency line had been long, but at last, Laney had managed to get through to someone. They had informed Laney that while they were indeed short-staffed, a deputy would come by to make out a report sometime in the next few hours. Laney hung up the phone triumphantly. *See, Diane, they can always make time for actual law enforcement*, she thought. Then she found herself wondering once again if Diane had known that all along, and had just been trying to discourage Laney from calling the sheriff at all.

Don't be suspicious, she chided herself. *Leave it to the police to figure out.*

With the call to the sheriff taken care of, Laney and Suze turned their attention to calling the ticket-holders for the fashion show who hadn't provided an e-mail address. While there wasn't an overly large number of these, getting through the list took more than a few hours. Every person Laney called wanted to talk about the fire, ask about Laney's family, and fill her in on the details of their own:

"My nephew down in Fernhill had to leave everything behind, and he barely escaped with his life! He said that as he drove away, there were flames chasing him down the road. It's true!"

"My daughter decided to preemptively evacuate, and she went to Portland. Can you believe it? Portland! I asked her why she'd ever want to go there, and she was just insistent that everywhere else is going to run out of hotel space. Well, I know that the Penngrove is all booked up, but there are plenty of good hotels in Yakima, you don't have to go to Portland."

"I don't care what they say, I'm not evacuating. My granddaddy was born in this house, and my daddy was born in this house, and I was born in this house, and I will not be leaving this house until they carry me out in a pine box."

Laney winced, putting the receiver down and crossing another name off the list. She was just about to dial the next number when her cell phone buzzed on the desk beside her. Carmen. She set down the ticket-holder list and picked up her cell.

"Carmen, are you okay? I heard they evacuated most of Fernhill."

"Yeah, Claudia and I had to leave," Carmen said. She sounded exhausted. "We tried to check in at the Penngrove, but they're full. They said that the Bible Fellowship has some space for evacuees to shelter, but we've got Sofia with us." Sofia was Carmen and Josh's regal blue point Ragdoll cat.

"Oh, poor baby, she must be terrified," Laney said.

"She is. She's huddled in the back of her carrier and she's not speaking to me." Carmen sighed. "I don't know what to do, Laney. I can't keep her in this carrier for days. I guess we're going to have to find somewhere out of town to stay. I never thought I'd say this, but I'm starting to regret moving so far from civilization. Everywhere we could go is more than an hour away, and I hate to go so far from our house. I'd kind of wanted to keep tabs on it."

"What about my apartment?" Laney suggested. "I've got a sleeper sofa in my living room. Would you and Claudia mind sharing a bed?"

"Seriously?" Carmen asked. "You really wouldn't mind?"

"Of course not," Laney said sincerely. "I mean, I don't know how long we'll be able to stay there ourselves, or if we'll have to evacuate, too. But at least then you won't be alone. Have you been able to get ahold of Josh?"

"Yeah," Carmen said. Her voice sounded sticky, and she sniffled before clearing her throat. "He's taking the next flight back, but it doesn't leave for a good twelve hours. The shortest flight he could find still won't get him back before Monday night. And I'm not sure if he'll even be able to get to us, what with the highways being closed."

"We'll play it by ear," Laney said soothingly. "If we haven't been evacuated by that point, there are ways around. Even if it takes a few extra hours, we'll get you to PDX."

"Thank you, Laney," Carmen said, her voice sounding sticky again.

"No problem. I'm at the museum right now, but if you come by the office I can get you the keys to the store and the apartment."

Laney had just sent Carmen and Claudia on their way when the doorbell rang. She hurried up the stairs and down the hall to the front door. A deputy wearing a khaki-and-forest-green uniform and an N95 mask stood on the porch. "I got a call about a possible break-in?" he said.

"Well, actually, I didn't see any evidence of a break-in," Laney admitted. In fact, that was another odd thing about this whole situation—the alarm hadn't gone off at all, and she hadn't noticed any signs of forced entry. Not that she'd looked too closely, though. "But at least two of our paintings appear to have been stolen."

"Appear to be?" the deputy repeated.

"Yes. Well, you see, they were replaced with copies," Laney explained.

"And you're sure that they're not the originals?" the man asked.

"I'm positive," Laney said, bristling. "I wouldn't have called you if I wasn't."

The deputy's eyebrows shot up, and Laney took a deep breath—which probably would have been more soothing if smoky air wasn't leaking in through the open door. *More flies with honey,* she reminded herself.

"Here, come in out of that smoke and let me show you," she said in a friendlier voice.

The air in the entryway was still hazy, but the deputy removed his mask once Laney had shut the door. She led him into the parlor where the Victorian lady's portrait hung. As she had with Paul the day before, she pulled out her phone and zoomed in on the tear in the corner.

"See, it's gone," Laney said. "Our collections manager confirmed that we haven't had this painting repaired. She also agreed with me that the paintings appear to have been swapped out with copies."

The deputy made some notations in a spiral notepad. "Is it all right with you if I take a look around the house for any signs of forced entry?"

"Of course," Laney said, feeling relieved. So he was taking her seriously after all. The police would get to the bottom of this in no time.

"And I'll need to talk to your collections manager as well."

"Sure thing. She's in the office downstairs. I can send her up here."

"No, I'll go down with you. The office is in a daylight basement, right?" the deputy asked.

"Right. The house was built into a hill; the ground is higher on the north and east sides than it is on the south and west," Laney explained. "There aren't any external doors in the basement, but there are several full-size windows."

"So there are more possible points of entry down there. I'll want to check those out as well."

The deputy was at the house for a little over an hour. While he was there, Laney tried to keep herself occupied by calling more ticket-holders, but she couldn't focus. After investigating all the possible points of entry, he'd taken Suze into the bridal room for privacy to get her statement, but Laney could still hear bits and pieces of their conversation from across the hall, which kept her from being able to concentrate.

At last, Suze emerged, the officer following behind her. "I'll be in touch when I know more," he said to Suze.

"Wait, are you leaving?" Laney asked. "Don't you want to take a statement from me?"

"I think I have all the information I need for now. It's not exactly a murder investigation," the deputy said with a wry grin. "But if I find I have any questions, I'll be sure to get in touch."

Laney glowered as Suze walked the deputy to the door. When she returned, Laney pounced on her. "So? What did he say?"

"He said that you were right—there didn't seem to be any signs of forced entry. But that doesn't mean anything. I told him that we leave the doors unlocked for self-guided tours on the days we don't have volunteer docents to lead official tours. He said it's a wonder we haven't had more things stolen."

Laney scoffed. "Do you seriously think someone could have brought in a duplicate painting, swapped it with the original, and left without anybody noticing? That landscape painting is ten feet away from Diane's office door!"

Suze shrugged, frowning. "I mean, anything's possible. Maybe it happened on a day Diane was out. Or maybe she was on the phone, or in a meeting, or talking to Viv."

Laney pressed on undeterred. "How would some random stranger have been able to make such a good copy of the paintings, anyway?"

"Well, there are images of our collection online," Suze pointed out. "Or someone could have taken a picture of them with their phone, the way you did with that portrait. If it was good enough for you to make a replica dress, it would probably be good enough for someone to make a replica painting."

Laney still felt skeptical, but it's not exactly like she had any better answers. She sighed. "So what do we do now?"

"He told me to do an inventory of the rest of the collection and make sure nothing else is missing. He'll be back to do a more thorough investigation once the fire situation is resolved."

Laney's eyes bugged. "*After* the fire? But who knows how long that could be! It can take weeks to get a fire fully contained—months! If we wait that long, the thief's trail will be cold!"

"We don't know how long ago the paintings were swapped to begin with," Suze pointed out. "The trail could already be cold. He told me that most of the time in cases like this, the thief is never found, anyway. We're probably just going to have to file a claim with our insurance and move on. At least the thief was nice enough to give us copies we can leave on display."

Laney didn't think that was *nice* in the least. And she refused to accept the possibility that the paintings had been gone for more than a few days. The fae would have alerted her to it sooner. They knew what was going on; they probably had even seen who'd done it. If only she could *see* them better! If only she could *talk* to them! They'd tell her exactly who to look for.

"We can't just display copies as if they're the real thing," she said sourly.

"Of course not," Suze said. "But we could make a notation on the caption placard, explaining that the original was stolen. It's better than nothing," she added as Laney's glower deepened.

"I suppose," Laney muttered.

Maybe Suze was willing to accept what the deputy said, that the thief would likely never be found. But not Laney. She knew that those paintings still had to be nearby. They couldn't have been gone for more than a few days. They might still even be in town. But they wouldn't stay that way for long, especially if Foreston were to be evacuated. No, this definitely couldn't wait. If the thief was going to be caught, they would have to find him or her as quickly as possible.

And if the police weren't going to do it, then Laney would do it herself.

Chapter 9

Laney frowned as she opened the front door to leave the museum. The air was hazy, the sky faded from the bizarre orange of this morning to a lighter yellow as the sun climbed higher overhead. She shut the door quickly to keep smoke from getting into the house, and was starting to rummage through her purse for the mask Taryn had given her when she heard a man's voice call her name.

She started, turning to see Paul standing at the bottom of the porch steps, a respirator over his mouth and nose. Flustered, she pulled her own mask on and descended the stairs to join him. She felt different than she had yesterday, somehow. Less volatile. Shyer.

He kept your number. After everything that happened when you left.

"Paul," she said, hoping her voice didn't shake. "What are you doing here?"

"Just wanted to check in and see how you're holding up," he replied. "I reckon the fashion show's been canceled?"

Laney nodded. "I just finished calling all the ticket-holders to notify them."

"That's too bad. I know you put a lot of work into it."

"Yeah, well." Laney shrugged, trying—and failing—to seem unaffected. "I think everybody's plans were thrown off by this, not just mine. We can reschedule when this is all over." *If the Paine Estate is still standing, that is.*

Paul seemed to have the same thought, but he was gracious enough not to say it. "How's everyone else at the museum holding up?" He lowered his voice and added, "Were you able to talk to the collections manager about those paintings?"

She nodded, hesitating. She glanced back up at the front door, and then steered him away from the house, into the shade of the large yew. "I did, and we called the sheriff. Diane was really mad about it."

Paul's thick brows furrowed. "Mad about the paintings being stolen?"

"No, mad about us calling the sheriff," Laney whispered. "Don't you think that's weird?"

He glanced back over his shoulder in the direction of the house. "That does sound rather odd. What did the sheriff have to say?"

"A deputy came out and made a report, but he said they won't be able to follow up on the investigation until the fire's out," Laney said.

"Fair enough," said Paul. "Or—I take it you don't agree?" he added as Laney's face fell.

"I understand *why*," Laney admitted, "but I don't like it. This fire is a perfect cover-up for the thief to get away with the paintings, and if that happens, we'll never see them again. The deputy himself even told us that we probably wouldn't be able to get them back."

Paul watched her silently. His expression was hard to read with the mask covering the lower half of his face. "This is really important to you," he said at last.

Laney looked away from him, her face hot. "It's just... I..." She took a step away from him, looking up at the branches of the tree above her. The leaves rustled slightly, though yesterday's wind had died down significantly. She squinted; she could just barely make out a humanoid shadow moving along the branch above her. No doubt laughing at her discomfort. "Those paintings belonged to the original family who lived here. We don't have a lot of their things. They were sold after their daughter died without an heir. Having those paintings in our collection, in the house where they hung for over a hundred years... It was just really special. I hate the idea of some thief taking that away from us."

Paul nodded thoughtfully. "And did the deputy give you any leads at all?"

Laney shook her head. "He said there was no sign of a break-in. However it is that the thief managed to switch the paintings, they don't seem to have broken into the house to do so." She frowned, chewing her lip. "He seemed to think that those paintings were stolen a long time ago and we just never noticed. That the trail is cold now. But I *know* they couldn't have been gone for more than a few days, Paul. I couldn't have missed it for longer than that. *They* wouldn't have let me—" She broke off abruptly. She hadn't meant to blurt that out. She scrambled to think of a change of subject, but Paul was there on the jump.

"*They?*" he asked, his eyebrow raised.

"No one," Laney said quickly, looking away from him.

He took a step forward, directly into her line of sight, and held her gaze. "The fae?" he asked.

Laney's eyes widened. "You remembered," she said in surprise.

"How could I forget?" Paul said, creases forming around his eyes with the grin his mask concealed.

Laney smiled herself, feeling her cheeks grow hot. Paul watched her, his expression sobering. "Laney, listen," he said. "We need to talk. That night—"

Laney involuntarily sucked in a breath of air and then choked on it. Even with the respirator covering her mouth, smoke was everywhere. She coughed violently, waving Paul away when he moved forward to pound her back.

"Sorry," she said when the coughing had finally subsided. "We probably should get out of this smoke. It can't be good for either of us." She squeezed her eyes shut, praying that her coughing fit would be enough to get him off the subject of that night, or her last week in London in general.

Paul's shoulders slumped, just a little. "Right," he murmured. He moved out of the shade of the yew tree, the shrouded sun casting strange shadows over his face. "But Laney, listen. Maybe I can help you with the paintings."

She looked up at him quizzically. "You can?"

He shrugged. "Well, maybe. I've done some investigative work in my time, as you may recall. I could help you go through the records, through the list of volunteers, see if we can find any sort of clue."

"The volunteer list?" Laney repeated.

Paul nodded. "If there's no sign of a break-in, then the most likely scenario is that it's someone who works for the museum, be they staff or volunteer."

Laney frowned. "I can't believe anyone who works here would sabotage the museum like that."

"Humanity can surprise you," Paul replied, his voice dark. Laney's chest squeezed, and this time it had nothing to do with the smoke in the air. She knew he'd probably seen the worst people had to offer over the course of his career. Had he faced all of it alone? Or did he have someone to help him cope? Someone like that girl in the pub...

Don't think about it don't think about it don't think—

"Well, I would appreciate the help," she said, collecting herself. "That is, if you have time. I know you're supposed to be working..."

"No trouble. I've got to film the afternoon update on the fire in about twenty minutes, but then I'm free."

"Okay. I'm heading over to Friedman's to get some more of these," Laney said, tapping her mask with one finger.

"All right. Meet you back here in an hour?" Paul asked.

"Sounds good," said Laney.

Just over an hour later, the doorbell rang. Laney had gotten back with the respirators and some lunch for herself some time before, but she'd barely managed to make a dent in her sandwich. Her thoughts were a jumble. Accepting Paul's help had probably been a huge mistake, especially given that she'd only just managed to escape having a Serious Discussion with him by her coughing fit. *You're supposed to be* avoiding *him*, she reminded herself.

But she couldn't deny that having someone with Paul's

investigative experience helping the museum was the next best thing to the sheriff himself. If she wanted to catch the art thief before they escaped, she couldn't pass up any offer of assistance. This fire had left her feeling especially helpless. But if she could find and return the paintings to the museum, she'd feel like she'd been able to accomplish *something*, and that had to be better than just sitting around worrying.

Laney answered the door, but before Paul could speak, she placed a finger to her lips. "Diane," she mouthed silently, gesturing in the direction of her office.

Paul nodded, pulling off his mask and following her quietly to the stairs down to the basement. After she closed the stairway door, Paul whispered, "You don't want her to know I'm here?"

"You know she'd freak out about it," Laney whispered. "Look how she reacted when we said we were going to call the sheriff."

Paul nodded thoughtfully but didn't reply.

Suze looked up as Laney and Paul entered the office, her eyes widening as she recognized Paul. "Hi," she squeaked after a moment of opening and closing her mouth without success.

"Nice to meet you. Paul Nelson," Paul said, leaning across the desk to shake her hand.

"Yeah, um... I recognize you from the TV. Laney didn't mention you'd be coming back by." Suze shot Laney a look. Laney shifted awkwardly. "Are you still proceeding with the travel segment, even with the fire?" Suze asked.

"Oh, no, no," Paul said. "Laney told me about your missing painting problem, so I volunteered to help you get some information together for the sheriff. Take a look at the records, see if there's anything that stands out as a potential 'clue,' if you will." He smiled charmingly, and Laney tried not to roll her eyes as Suze visibly melted before him.

Junior year all over again, she thought.

"Oh, that's so generous of you," Suze gushed.

"Not at all. I honestly don't know how much help I can be to you at all, but I reckoned I'd give it a go. Could I get a copy of your volunteer roster?"

"Of course," Suze said, turning to her computer to pull the Excel file up. "So, are you staying in town even with everything else going on?"

"Yeah, the network wants to keep me here to cover the fire as long as possible. Since I was already in town when it broke out, they were able to get a jump on the story before the other news networks."

Laney winced. "That's a bit of a mercenary attitude to have about a natural disaster," she said.

Paul gave her a look she couldn't quite read. Almost raw, like he'd had the thought himself so many times that it had worn him thin. "Welcome to the wonderful world of cable news," he said.

Laney frowned, but before she could ask him to elaborate, Suze said, "So, do you have the latest scoop on the fire? How close is it to town?"

"It's still a ways off, fortunately," Paul replied. "The winds died down overnight, which helped a lot in slowing the spread and helping the firefighters make some headway in containing it."

"That's great news," Laney said. "Do you think they'll have it out soon?"

"I wouldn't go that far. The last I heard, they'd had some success implementing control lines, but it's still less than ten percent contained. A lot could change, especially if the wind picks up again."

"Well, hopefully it won't spread as far as Foreston," Suze said as the printer spat out three pages of names. She removed them from the tray and handed them to Paul. "Is there anything else I can get you?"

"If I could get a look at the insurance records on your art collection, that would be great," Paul said, giving the volunteer roster a cursory glance before folding the papers and putting them in his back pocket.

"The insurance records?" Laney asked.

Paul nodded. "That will give us an idea of what value they're appraised at. Plus, usually that paperwork will include photos and detailed descriptions about any particular features the artwork may possess. You recognized that missing portrait based on the tear in the corner, right, Laney? Characteristics like that will be noted on the paperwork. We can use that information to make sure that no other artwork in the museum is missing."

"That's a great idea," Suze said. "I didn't even think of that. I haven't started my inventory yet, so that will get us out ahead of the game. The files are back this way." She climbed awkwardly over the mess that littered the office floor—boxes of files, boxes of collections items, rolled-up carpets, and an old copy machine that hadn't worked for a good five years—and pulled open the drawer.

Laney winced, looking at Paul. "Sorry about the mess."

"Not at all," Paul said with a laugh. "I've seen my fair share of museum offices over the years. They all look like this, if not worse."

"Laney, can you come look at this?" Suze asked. Her voice sounded weird, almost strangled. Laney followed the path she'd taken through the obstacle course of junk and looked over her shoulder into the open file cabinet drawer. "I can't find the insurance files," Suze said in a low voice.

"Are you sure they didn't get put back in the wrong drawer?" Laney asked. It had been known to happen. Frequently.

"I don't think so," Suze said. "The folders are here, see?" She pulled out a stack of manila tab folders, each labeled with a particular painting's title. She flipped one open, then another. All empty. "I don't think someone would have put the folders back without the paperwork in them."

A knot curled in Laney's stomach as the meaning of Suze's words hit her. "So you're saying..."

Suze bit her lip, looking back down at the file cabinet. "I think someone took them."

Chapter 10

"I still just don't understand," Laney said as she and Paul left the house. It was evening by now, the smoky sky turning dark. They'd combed the office for hours, just in case the paperwork had been misplaced, but it was nowhere to be found. "Why would someone take the insurance paperwork?"

"My best guess is they did it to muddy the waters, make it harder for anyone who wasn't intimately familiar with the artwork's distinguishing characteristics to prove that the forgeries are not the originals," Paul suggested. "I suspect most people—even museum staff—haven't studied the paintings with as much of an eye to detail as you did with that portrait, and that was an unusual circumstance. You'd never have noticed at all if they'd swapped the painting before you took that picture on your phone."

And if the fae hadn't warned me, Laney thought. Then she

froze on the bottom step of the porch, her hand instinctively shooting out to grab Paul's arm and gripping it so tightly that her fingernails dug through the fabric of his jacket.

"Ow!" he exclaimed.

"Paul," she hissed as he detached himself from her claws. "That proves it! The painting hadn't been swapped yet when I took that photo. That gives us a time frame for when the theft took place." She yanked her phone out of her purse, swiping until she'd pulled the photo up yet again. She tapped to see the date and time it had been taken. "This was just under a month ago."

"So the paintings must have been stolen within the last month," Paul said. "Have any of the museum staff or docents quit over the last month?"

"No," Laney said.

"Which means whoever the thief is, they still work here."

Laney frowned behind her mask. "Are you positive it's one of the volunteers? I can't believe any of them would do that."

"It must be, Laney. You could argue that anyone could come in while the museum is unlocked, but only volunteers and staff have access to that office. That's something that *would* be much too hard for an outsider to pull off without anyone noticing."

Laney's shoulders slumped. "I guess you're right," she admitted.

"What about Vivian, the museum director?" Paul said. "You

did say she's in Mexico now."

Laney scoffed. "Are you seriously suggesting that Viv is on the lam right now?" Paul snickered, and she shot him a glare. "What?"

"'*On the lam*'," Paul laughed.

"Isn't that the right phrase?"

"Oh, it is. It's just hilarious to hear you say it."

"Why, because I'm not a big, tough journalist like you?" Laney crossed her arms.

Paul laughed again. "I'm just teasing you, Laney," he said, nudging her elbow. She crossed her arms even tighter, trying to ignore the tingle that was now shooting up her right arm.

"What about Diane?" she suggested.

Paul nodded thoughtfully. "Could be. You did say she behaved suspiciously when you told her about the theft. But we shouldn't jump to any conclusions. We need more evidence."

"But how are we going to get it with the insurance records missing? We can't even dust for fingerprints on those file folders—all three of us touched them, and I'm sure half the people in our office have, too."

"Well—" Paul began, but he broke off when a chime rang out. He pulled his phone out of his jeans pocket, quickly scanning the message that had just come in. Then he looked up at her. "I'm sorry, Laney, I didn't realize how late it had gotten. Can we table this until tomorrow? I have a conference call with my producers, and then I need to film the evening segment before I head over to the Bible Fellowship."

"The Bible Fellowship?" Laney repeated. "Why are you going there?"

Paul looked down, putting his phone back in his pocket and avoiding her eyes. "They've got a shelter set up for people without a place to stay during evacuation."

"Right, but you have a place to stay. You had a room at the Penngrove, right?"

"Um, well..." He shifted uncomfortably before finally meeting her eyes, sheepish. "This older woman came in, and they were out of rooms. She had her dog with her, a little corgi like the ruddy queen. And I thought, I can't make her sleep on a cot in a church hall."

"You gave up your room?" Laney said, her demeanor softening.

"It's not a big deal, honestly," Paul said quickly. "I've slept on a lot worse than a cot." His phone chimed again. "Sorry, I really need to go." He hesitated, looking at her earnestly. "Talk to you tomorrow?"

She stared at him for a long moment. Even in the semidarkness, his blue eyes were magnetic. As he turned to go, she heard herself saying, "Paul, wait." He paused, turning back to her. Without giving herself a chance to think it over, she blurted out, "You don't have to stay at the Bible Fellowship. Seriously. I have a sleeper couch in my living room. You're welcome to stay there."

His brows rose high on his forehead. "No, I couldn't—"

"I insist. And it will open up a cot at the church for evacuees," Laney pointed out.

Paul hesitated for a long moment, his eyes fixed on Laney's. "All right," he said finally. "That would be highly appreciated. I should be done around ten o'clock."

"Perfect," Laney said. "My apartment's over the store. Text me when you get there and I'll let you in."

He held her gaze a minute longer. "Thank you, Laney," he said softly. Then his phone chimed yet again. "All right, I'm off," he said with an apologetic wave. She watched his form disappear into the shadows.

"Laney McCarthy," she said to herself when he was gone. "You are an absolute idiot."

Chapter 11

"Excuse me?" Claudia stared at Laney incredulously. "Are you telling me you double-booked your couch?"

"I'm sorry! I genuinely forgot!" Laney said. She'd already known she was in trouble the moment she blurted out that invitation before thinking it over more carefully. But she hadn't realized just how much trouble she was in.

After she and Paul had parted ways, Laney had wandered over to the Brownstone for dinner and wound up spending the entire time on the phone: first with her parents, and then Taryn, and then Matthew, who'd demanded to know why Laney hadn't forcibly removed their parents from their home and driven them down to Eugene herself. She'd had to remind him that even though she'd closed the shop, she'd still had a ton of work at the museum with the cancellation of the fashion show—she neglected to mention the part about the stolen paintings and her own private investigation of said theft, lest Matthew *really* blow a gasket—and, she pointed out, what did he expect her to do, strong-arm them? That had led to an even bigger argument, because, yes, Matthew did indeed expect her to strong-arm them. By the time she'd finally hung up on her brother, the next thing she'd known, the evening news was on, and she *did* need to keep abreast of what was going on, after all. Unfortunately, her eye kept drifting over to the TV that Paul's broadcast was on, which just tangled her mind into further knots.

The good news was that the fire hadn't yet jumped the firefighters' control line. The bad news was that the wind was scheduled to pick up again on Monday night, so if they didn't get it further contained by then, it could continue to spread.

The worst news was that by the time Laney pried herself away from the Brownstone, it was already after nine. That would have been plenty of time to get the apartment ready for her house guest... if she hadn't forgotten that she already *had* two. Well, three if you counted Sofia, who'd been freed from her carrier and was currently hiding under Laney's antique secretary desk, the tip of her long, fluffy tail peeking out between the wooden feet.

"Maybe all three of us would fit on the sleeper," Laney suggested, but even as the words came out of her mouth, she knew it would be impractical. The sofa comfortably accommodated two, but trying to squeeze three adults onto that bed would leave them crammed in as tightly as sardines, and Laney wasn't sure it could hold that much weight.

"Doubtful," said Claudia. "Maybe if you've got a king-sized bed in your room, the three of us could fit on that?"

Laney shook her head. "It's a double. It's even smaller than the sofa bed." She sighed. "I'm just going to have to send him on his way."

"No, don't do that," Carmen said. "He already had to give up his hotel room. And I heard the Bible Fellowship is low on cots. What's going to happen if they don't have any more space? Do you want him to have to sleep on a bench, out there in all that smoke?"

Laney sighed. "Of course not. I guess I'll sleep on the floor." She gestured to the pile of cushions on the floor that had been removed from the sofa in order to open the bed up. "These spread out would make a nice mattress. He can have my room."

"Are you sure?" Carmen asked. "I could be the one to sleep on the floor."

"Absolutely not," Laney said firmly. "You two are my guests. I'm the one who messed up. You are not sleeping on the floor."

Carmen nodded, and the three of them looked around the living room in silence. From under the secretary desk, Sofia's tail twitched.

"Laney," Carmen said quietly, "are you ever going to tell us what happened between you and Paul? It seems a bit more...

complicated than you originally let on."

Laney could *feel* her cheeks turning red. "How so?"

"I don't know. You said the two of you broke up, but every time I've seen you together, it feels more... unresolved than that. More like... I don't know. Like you're just on pause or something. I mean, I don't think that Claudia would offer to let her ex-husband stay on her sleeper sofa."

"Oh, heck no," Claudia said. "That worm could sleep on the park bench, smoke or no smoke."

"It was amicable," Laney lied. Even as she said it, her mind flashed with the memory of that night at the pub. She swallowed, blinking it away. "I was moving back to the US, he was staying in England. It seemed impractical to try to keep things going long-distance."

"But he's here now," Carmen pointed out. "He lives in the US."

"Yeah, in New York," Laney said, remembering the area code on his cell phone. "That's still long-distance. It's on the opposite side of the country."

"He's a field reporter. It's not like he's filming in a studio," said Claudia. "With all the traveling he has to do, I doubt it matters where he lives."

"I don't even know if he's single," Laney protested. "And I'm not looking to get back with him, okay? We broke up for a reason."

"And what is the reason, Laney?" Carmen asked. "The *real* reason."

Laney bit her lip. She was cornered. "I..."

Her phone buzzed loudly on the table beside the front door. She started, then hurried over to grab it, grateful to derail this conversation. "He's here," she said. "I need to go let him in."

She hurried down the stairs into the darkened store, pulling the apartment door closed behind her so Sofia wouldn't escape—not that she appeared to be planning on coming out from under the secretary desk any time soon. Through the glass storefront, she could see Paul standing at the front door, a respirator covering his mouth and nose, a duffel bag slung over his shoulder.

"Hey," she said, flipping on the lights and opening the door.

"You sure you haven't changed your mind?" he asked, hesitating on the sidewalk.

"I'm sure. Come in," Laney said. She closed and locked the door behind him while he removed his mask and glanced around the store. "We do have a bit of an overcrowding issue, though," she added, gesturing for him to follow her up the stairs.

"I'm sorry?" Paul said.

By way of answer, Laney opened the apartment door and gestured to Carmen and Claudia.

"I forgot that I'd already made a reservation for my sleeper couch earlier today. Carmen—oh, sorry, and this is her sister,

Claudia—they live in Fernhill. They got evacuated, so I told them they could stay here with their kitty."

Paul blinked at them for a confused moment, then quickly said, "I'm terribly sorry, I didn't realize. I can head over to the church—"

"No, no, we figured it out already. I'm going to sleep on the floor." She pointed to the nest of couch cushions. "And you can have my room."

"I can't ask you to do that, Laney," Paul protested.

"Seriously, I insist," she replied. "I'm the one who messed up, after all."

"I am not going to be able to rest if I know you're sleeping on the floor."

"It's just for a couple nights. Carmen's husband will be back from the UAE on Monday," Laney explained. "If the fire is still an issue after that, we can play it by ear."

Paul looked from Laney to Carmen and Claudia—watching with visible interest—to Sofia's tail hanging out from under the secretary desk. "All right," he finally said. "But I'll be the one to sleep on the floor."

"Paul—" Laney began, but he cut her off.

"*I* insist. I refuse to let the three of you *completely* emasculate me."

Laney felt the corners of her mouth twitching upward in spite of herself. "Okay," she said. "But"—she lowered her voice to almost a whisper—"I don't think you should sleep out here. That might make them uncomfortable."

"We can hear you, you know," Claudia said. "But you're not wrong."

Paul laughed. "Understandable. I can sleep down in the store if you'd like."

"No, don't do that," Laney said. "There are a million things you could trip over down there, and there's only the one light switch—you'll never be able to sleep with the place lit up like a Christmas tree. Plus, we've got a glass storefront. Anyone could look in and that would just creep me out."

"Okay, but..." Paul trailed off. If not in the living room, and not in the store, where could he go? The kitchen and the bathroom weren't big enough to spread the couch cushions out, which just left—

Laney sighed. "You can sleep in my room," she said.

"Honestly, Laney," Paul said, "you don't have to do that. I can still head over to the church—"

She shook her head firmly, trying to ignore the flabbergasted expressions that Carmen and Claudia were giving her. "It's fine. Come on, I'll get you set up."

She felt oddly self-conscious as she opened the door to her bedroom and flipped on the light switch. Fortunately, she'd made her bed before leaving for the museum that morning—something she didn't always do—so at least the room was tidy. But she still felt strange, letting a guy see her room. Especially since that guy was Paul.

"There should be room for the cushions here," Laney said, gesturing to a spot on the floor next to her dresser.

Paul looked around her room with some interest, which made her feel like she was under a microscope. He'd seen her room in the student halls, of course, but she hadn't brought much with her for her year abroad, so it had been more impersonal. Here, everything—from the photos on her dresser to her blue paisley bedspread and curtains to the paint color on the wall—reflected her own taste. She felt a little exposed.

Especially when he gestured to her bed and laughed, "You have an impressive collection of throw pillows going on there. You could make a formidable pillow fort with those."

Laney's face burned, but she couldn't help laughing herself. "Interesting that that's where your mind went."

Paul shrugged. "I am nothing if not juvenile."

"Okay, well, make yourself comfortable," Laney said. "I'm going to go shut the lights off downstairs and set the alarm. I hope you're not planning on trying to escape in the night, because the whole neighborhood will know and my reputation will be ruined by morning."

"I wouldn't dream of it," Paul replied, his voice solemn despite the smirk on his face. "Heaven forfend I impugn your honor." He was still snickering as she left her room, shaking her head in an attempt to conceal her own inability to keep a straight face.

By the time she'd finished up downstairs, Carmen and Claudia had changed into their pajamas and were curled up on the sofa bed, the TV on in the corner.

"Do you two want an extra blanket?" Laney asked as she squeezed past them through the narrow space the opened bed left in her small living room.

"No, thanks. It's stuffy in here with the windows closed," Carmen replied.

"Tell me about it," Laney said, opening the linen closet and pulling out a set of sheets for Paul to cover the couch cushions with. She tried not to think too hard about her selection. She felt self-conscious about everything she was doing.

"Have a good night," Claudia called in a sing-song voice. Carmen burst into giggles beside her as Laney ground her teeth, shutting the closet door a little more forcefully than was strictly necessary. She stormed down the hall and then took a deep breath to compose herself before going back into her room.

"I brought some sheets if you want them," she said as she came through the door. Paul had changed into a white T-shirt, but he was still wearing his jeans.

"Ah, thank you," he said, taking the fitted sheet and tucking it around the cushions.

"Are you going to sleep in your jeans?" Laney asked.

"I reckon you'd be uncomfortable if I slept without them."

Laney rolled her eyes. "The bathroom is in the hall if you want to put on pajamas." When he just stared at her, she sighed. "Let me guess—you don't own any pajamas."

Paul shrugged. "Living the bachelor life."

He watched her intently for a moment, and she felt the self-consciousness come creeping back over her. She climbed over the couch cushions and rummaged through her dresser for the most matronly pair of pajamas she owned. "Well, I'm going to change into mine, at least," she announced, escaping to the bathroom.

She took her time brushing her teeth, washing her face, and combing her hair. She even managed a messy braid, something that she hadn't done in a while. She was stalling. She knew it. Was it too late to make a run for it? Maybe she could go back to her parents' house tonight and let her guests have the run of the apartment. But that wouldn't be fair to Carmen and Claudia. And then she definitely wouldn't be able to hide the fact that Paul was staying at her apartment from Taryn. Not that she had much hope of keeping it from her sister, anyway—odds were high that Carmen or Claudia had already texted her the news. But still, if there was even a *chance...*

She sighed. There was no point staying in here any longer. She'd made her bed, now she'd just have to lie in it.

When she returned to her room, Paul was sitting on the pile of cushions with his back against her dresser, tapping away on his phone. He looked up as Laney came in.

"Hey, roomie," he said, setting his phone down on the cushion beside him. "I was starting to worry you'd flushed yourself."

"You think this is just hilarious, don't you?" She went over to the bed and started stripping the throw pillows off, tossing them into the cedar trunk she kept at the foot of her bed. "I was considering sleeping in the bathtub. Maybe I still will."

"What, and miss out on the slumber party?" Paul teased. Laney threw a pillow at his head, but he shot a hand up quickly to catch it. "See, the pillow fights have already started! Maybe we can paint each other's nails next." Beside him, his phone buzzed, the screen lighting up.

"Are you texting your girlfriend? I doubt she's happy about you staying at your ex's apartment." The words were out of Laney's mouth before she'd even had a chance to think.

Paul's eyebrows rose in surprise. "What makes you think I have a girlfriend?"

Laney didn't look at him. She threw another pillow into the trunk. "Well, do you?"

Paul was quiet until she finally dared a glance in his direction. His expression was... complicated. "I do not," he said. "But I appreciate your concern for my nonexistent significant other's feelings."

"Oh," Laney said. A strange sensation was twisting its way out of her stomach. "You're welcome, I guess."

After a moment's awkward pause, Paul said, "Well, what about you? Don't you need to call your boyfriend?"

Laney chewed on the inside of her cheek. "You know perfectly well I don't have one."

She shot another glance in his direction. He was smiling. "What makes you think I know that?" he asked.

"I don't know. What makes you think that I don't have one?"

He held her eyes. "The fact that he's not here right now, but I am."

Her face was burning, and she knew from the grin on his face that he could see it. Annoyed, she turned away. "Maybe I have someone like Carmen's husband. Maybe he's in the UAE right now, too."

"You said Carmen's husband is on his way home."

"Maybe he's on a remote research station in Antarctica and can't be reached."

"That's probably it." There was laughter in his voice.

The room fell silent as Laney finished tossing pillows into the trunk and pulled back her bedspread. She stood beside her bed, staring at it with her arms crossed. There was absolutely zero chance that she would be able to sleep tonight.

"Laney, listen," Paul said quietly behind her. "We really need to talk."

She felt like a bucket of ice water had been dumped over her. Those words alone were enough to make her want to run.

Just like you did five years ago, huh? her mind whispered.

In a panic, she blurted, "No, honestly. I don't think we do." When Paul's brows furrowed, she hurriedly went on, "It was five years ago. We've both grown up and moved on. Our lives have gone in two totally separate directions, and I don't know about you, but I'm happy with my life. Well, apart from this fire, anyway," she added, gesturing vaguely in the direction of the window. Paul was watching her, but she couldn't read his expression. Desperately, she said, "So can we both just agree to keep the past in the past and move forward?"

He looked down, absently picking at a loose thread on the fitted sheet. "If that's what you want."

"It is."

"All right, then." He wouldn't look at her. "I won't bring it up again."

Relief washed over her, followed immediately by a wave of guilt. But why should she feel guilty? This would be better for both of them. There was no sense in reopening old wounds. "Okay. Sounds good," she said.

He didn't say anything as he plugged his phone into its charger and adjusted the pillow she'd given him for his head. "Well, I've got an early day tomorrow," he finally said, rolling onto his side, his back to Laney.

"Yeah. Me too," Laney replied. Her stomach was all twisted in knots. Ordinarily she'd read for a little bit before trying to sleep, but she wasn't in the mood tonight. She turned off the light and stared at the ceiling in the darkness.

She couldn't sleep, of course. She listened to the sounds of Carmen and Claudia talking in the living room, and the faint murmur of the TV, and the rustle of denim on cotton as Paul shifted uncomfortably on the couch cushions. Eventually, the sounds from the living room faded away, but she was still awake, and she could tell from his fidgeting that Paul was as well.

Laney sighed, sitting up in bed and looking over at the shadowy lump on her floor. "Can't sleep?" she said to his silhouette.

"Not like you can, either."

"Are the cushions uncomfortable?"

He chuckled. "I may have oversold my ability to sleep on the floor."

Laney sighed, staring at the small slivers of light from the streetlamp outside coming in between the slats of her blinds. Then she stood up, switched on her bedside lamp, and opened up the trunk.

"What're you doing?" Paul asked, sitting up on his elbows to watch her.

"You can sleep on the bed," Laney said.

"No, no," he said firmly. "You are not sleeping on these cushions."

"I won't." She took a handful of throw pillows and laid them out down the middle of her bed. She mounded them up high, like a wall. "You keep to your side, I'll keep to mine."

Paul scoffed. "You can't be serious."

"Yes, I can. Er, I am. But if you prefer, you can stay on the floor. Last call."

He scrambled up onto his feet.

"Stay on your side, remember," Laney said warningly.

He held up three fingers. "Scout's honor."

"Okay. Maybe now both of us can get some sleep."

"Yes, ma'am. Thank you, ma'am."

Laney rolled her eyes, getting back into her side of the bed and quickly switching off the light before he could once again notice how red her face was. She kept her back to him, her heartbeat erratic, conscious of how loud her own breath sounded in her ears. *I am never going to be able to sleep,* she thought woefully. *No amount of concealer is going to cover the bags under my eyes.*

On the other side of the pillow wall, Paul's breathing grew quieter while Laney stared into the shadows, replaying their conversation over and over. *I'm an idiot,* she thought sourly. *And a coward. Glad to see nothing's changed in five years.*

She lay there, listening to the sound of his breathing until she couldn't keep her own eyes open any longer.

Chapter 12

Laney slowly drifted back into consciousness. She could smell smoke, muted but still detectable, particles that had managed to squeeze in through the closed windows and the heater vents. But there was something else, something closer. Warm and sort of spicy, and unmistakably familiar. Faded aftershave. She opened her eyes to find Paul's face just inches from hers. His jaw was lined with stubble, and a curl of light-brown hair had fallen askew over his left eye. It reminded her of the unruly style he'd worn his hair in back when they were in college. He was still asleep, breathing softly, his left arm slung over her. Her head had been against his chest as they slept.

That jerk, she thought incredulously. *I told him to stay on his side!* But as she cautiously scooted away from him, trying to extract herself from his arms without waking him up, she realized that Paul *was* on his side of the pillow barricade—she was the one who'd rolled over the top of it.

She crawled back over the mound of pillows and sat there a moment, watching his sleeping form in the dim dawn light that leaked through the closed blinds while her insides twisted themselves into knots. *I'm an idiot*, she thought, and once again she wasn't sure if her brain was referring to her actions of the past thirty-six hours, or if it went back further than that.

Over by the dresser, an alarm sounded abruptly. Laney flung herself down on her side of the bed, feigning sleep as Paul began to stir. As he got up to shut off the alarm, Laney opened her eyes again, stretching sleepily.

"Sorry," Paul said. "I forgot I'd set this for so early. We've got a staff meeting, and then I have to film the morning segment."

"It's fine," Laney replied. Her voice sounded sticky, and she cleared her throat. "I need to get up, anyway. It always takes me a while to wake up, and I've got church this morning."

Paul nodded, rummaging through his duffel bag and pulling out a clean pair of clothes. Laney went over to the window and turned the wand on the blinds. The morning light was faintly beige, nothing like the usual purple-blue of dawn. When she turned back, Paul was watching her. He scratched the back of his neck sheepishly. "Is there somewhere I can wash up?" he asked.

"Oh!" Laney said. "Yeah. You can use the shower. We're going to have to figure out a schedule for that, with four of us here for the time being." She'd need to get him a key before he left so that he could get back in when she wasn't around. She wasn't used to having company—especially so many people at once. *This fire has turned the whole world upside down,* she thought. *In more ways than one.*

"I'll be quick. Shouldn't use too much hot water," he said.

"No problem. It doesn't take the water that long to heat back up."

Paul nodded, getting to his feet but pausing before opening the door. "Thank you, Laney. For letting me stay here and... everything."

Laney perched on the edge of the bed, watching him go. "Don't thank me," she said quietly.

She couldn't tell whether he heard her or not.

Laney looked around the rows of pews, pulling off her respirator and tucking it into her purse. They said you weren't supposed to reuse these masks, but Friedman's had been running low, so she was trying to make them stretch as much as possible. The church was emptier than usual. People had been evacuating. She couldn't blame them. Apart from how awful the smoke was, a lot of people probably figured it was better to leave on their own terms rather than wait and risk a bottleneck if the fire spread quicker than expected. When she'd checked the news this morning, she found there'd been some panic in the night when the fire jumped the control line, but the firefighters had managed to beat it back. As long as the wind stayed low like it had been, they might be okay. But the forecast indicated that the wind was supposed to pick up again tomorrow evening, and that could be dangerous.

Taryn was already seated in the third row beside their parents. Laney squeezed in beside them.

"Hey," Taryn said when she sat down. "How are you holding up? I heard it was almost as crazy-busy at your place as it is at the Penngrove."

Laney's heart stopped. "Oh?" she squeaked.

"Yeah, you know. Carmen, Claudia, and a cat in your tiny apartment?"

Laney swallowed in relief. So Carmen hadn't spilled the beans... yet. "Yeah, no, it was fine. They were pretty quiet house guests. I barely noticed them."

"*Un*like the Penngrove, then," Taryn laughed.

Eager to change the subject away from her house guests, Laney leaned forward to look at her parents. "Matthew's not too happy with you two," she said.

"We're aware," Aden replied dryly.

"I told him that we are not driving five hours just to satisfy his paranoia," Nancy put in. "His apartment is smaller than yours is. Where would we all fit? Not to mention that Tucker is scared of Bailey." She shook her head. Matthew's Doberman, Tucker, was notoriously afraid of just about everything he encountered—including their parents' mellow golden retriever. "If the sheriff says we *have* to evacuate, that's one thing. But there's no sense leaving our home before we absolutely have to."

"A lot of people seem to think evacuating early is a good idea," Laney said, gesturing around at the half-empty church.

"Well, we're not like a *lot* of people," Nancy huffed.

"He just feels bad that he's stuck down in Eugene while all of us are here," Taryn said soothingly. "He's worried about you."

"Nobody made him move so far away," said Nancy. "He didn't have to go to U of O. He could have gone to Washington State like you and Taryn did."

"And saved us some money on out-of-state tuition," Aden added under his breath.

Laney rolled her eyes. "Your complaining about Matthew's out-of-state tuition is exactly *why* Taryn and I went to Washington State, remember?"

"Besides, you know how Matthew is," Taryn added. "When he gets it in his head that he's meant to go somewhere or do something, he does it."

Nancy opened her mouth to argue some more, but just then the organ roared to life, and around them people began standing for the opening processional. Laney whispered a silent *thank you* to the ceiling as her mother sniffed and opened her hymnbook.

She tried her best to focus during the service, but her brain was as tumultuous this morning as it had been the night before. When she looked at the fresco behind the altar, she thought about the missing paintings. When she looked at the candles on either side of it, she thought about the fire. When she caught glimpses of Taryn or her parents in her periphery, she wondered if Matthew was right—if maybe she *should* attempt to strong-arm them and haul them down to Eugene. When she saw the colored light cast by the stained glass window, she thought about the fae and the message they'd been trying to give her, made a thousand times more difficult to comprehend by her own accursedly poor Sight.

And when she looked at the sandy-brown hair on the guy sitting in the row ahead of them, she thought of Paul—even though every time he turned his head slightly and she saw his mustache, she reminded herself that it was just Mr. Jenkins, who was a good fifteen years her senior and taught music at the local elementary school.

At the end of the service, one of the cantors stood at the podium to the right of the altar to read the weekly announcements. "I don't have much for you this week. Mostly everything in the area has been canceled or closed, understandably," she said. "But we did receive a request from the Bible Fellowship, who as you may know has opened their church up as a refuge for evacuees. They are in need of extra sheets and blankets. Hard to believe, in this hot weather, but some people—older folks, especially—tend to run a bit cooler than others, and many people didn't have a chance to pack blankets for themselves in their hurry to evacuate."

Laney chewed on the inside of her cheek. She'd been feeling so helpless, from the fire to the theft at the museum. But this was a way she could definitely help. She'd just need to check her fabric inventory...

As the parishioners stood for the closing song, Laney tucked her hymnal into the pocket on the back of the pew. As soon as the service was over, she had work to do back at the shop.

A few hours later, she pulled into the Bible Fellowship's parking lot. In the trunk of her car was a stack of sheets and a second stack of blankets—not as many as she'd hoped, but she'd had to make do with the fabric she had on hand, much of which was unsuitable for bedding. Still, she'd had enough cotton to make ten flat sheets and enough fleece to make five blankets.

She'd whispered to herself as she sewed every stitch, praying, over and over, that what she willed over the fabric and thread would come true: *Keep these people safe. Stop the fire. Save their houses.* If ever she needed her faery blessing to work, the time was now.

Carrying the laundry basket with the sheets and blankets, Laney pushed open the swinging doors to the church with her shoulder and looked around the lobby. It was empty, but she could hear a cacophony of voices coming through the double doors to her right. She followed the sound into a large hall. Cots filled the space, suitcases and backpacks and duffel bags sitting next to them or open atop them. Some people were sitting on their cots, reading or browsing their phones, but mostly everyone was crowded around a table on the wall opposite the doors.

"Laney!" a woman's voice called, and Laney turned to see Barbara Morrison, one of the volunteers at the Paine Estate, approaching her. A cheery-faced woman in her mid-sixties, her husband was the pastor of the Bible Fellowship.

"Hi, Barb," Laney said. "I heard you needed more bedding, so..." She tipped the laundry basket to show her the contents.

"Oh, wonderful," Barb said. "Thank you so much."

"I'm sorry I couldn't bring more. This was all the fabric I had," Laney said apologetically.

"Nonsense. We appreciate any donation at all. This will help a lot of families."

Barb gestured for Laney to follow her up front, where boxes and bags of other donations were stacked together. As she set down the laundry basket, she looked around the hall and her eyes widened in surprise. The table that she'd noticed when she came in the door was piled high with sandwiches, small bags of chips, and water bottles—and distributing those sandwiches were none other than Paul and the *Around America* crew.

Barb followed Laney's gaze and smiled warmly. "Oh, isn't that nice? The people from the news station bought lunch for all the evacuees."

"That is nice," Laney replied automatically. "Very considerate."

"They're the ones who were supposed to be filming the segment on the museum, right?" Barb asked. "There have been so many news crews coming through the last two days, I wasn't sure who was who."

"Yeah." Laney swallowed. "Paul Nelson interviewed me on Friday. They were supposed to film the fashion show, too, but..."

Barb put her hand on Laney's shoulder. "I'm so sorry about the fashion show, Laney. I know how much work you put into it."

"It's fine," said Laney. "Hopefully all this will be over soon, and our lives can get back to normal."

Barb smiled sadly. "I don't know if we'll ever be able to go back to the way things were before. But we can make a new normal."

As she spoke, Paul glanced up and noticed Laney standing with Barb. He waved, and Laney waved back awkwardly.

"He's a handsome one, isn't he?" Barb remarked.

"Is he? I didn't notice."

Barb snorted. "Right. I'm sure you didn't. You know, I think they might be a little understaffed. Why don't you offer to give them a hand distributing the sandwiches?" She gave Laney a little wink.

Laney was about to make an excuse about how she had other things she needed to do, but the truth was, she didn't. She'd said she wanted to help out; true, she'd made the sheets and the blankets, but if she went home now, all she'd be able to do is worry. And she couldn't exactly avoid Paul, anyway. He was staying at her apartment. Her plan to hide from him for the duration of his stay in Foreston had long since gone out the window.

Besides, if she went home now, she'd have to field demanding questions from Carmen and Claudia about how the evening had gone.

That thought was what did it, in the end. She fished around her purse for a hair tie, pulling her long red hair back into a ponytail. She slipped her phone into her back pocket, left her purse with the other volunteers', and Barb brought her over to the table.

"Hey, Laney," Ashley said, glancing in her direction as she handed a water bottle to the man in front of her.

"Laney here said she'd like to help you hand out lunch," Barb said.

"Oh, great," Ashley replied. "Would you be willing to take over water duty? I'm thinking that if I can go down the line and get people's sandwich orders in advance, that might streamline things a little. We've got ham, turkey, and peanut butter-and-jelly," she explained.

"Sure," Laney said, taking Ashley's place at the table beside Paul.

"Hey, roomie," Paul said when Ashley and Barb had gone.

Laney blushed crimson. "Do you mind?" she hissed.

Paul laughed. "Not at all."

"Why do you enjoy picking on me so much?" Laney asked, handing a water bottle to an older woman with a long silver braid running down her back.

"How could you accuse me of that?" Paul said in mock offense. Then he added, "Your reaction makes it worth the while."

Laney glowered, passing another water bottle across the table.

Paul sobered and leaned closer, saying in a low voice, "I did some research on that list of names you gave me. Do you have time to talk about it when we're done here?"

Laney's heart beat faster, a combination of the thought of news about the case and Paul's proximity. "Yeah," she said.

"Brill. There are some classrooms in the basement. Meet me down there when lunch is over."

Chapter 13

Laney sighed, looking around the dim classroom. The frosted glass on the windows filtered the light that streamed in, almost letting Laney forget about the smoke outside. Here, she could pretend that it was just a typical gray Washington day, that it was just dim because of the clouds and not because of the world being on fire.

Almost.

The door to the classroom opened. "There you are," Paul said, coming to join her. She was sitting on the floor, her back against the wall, a chalkboard mounted above her head. When Ashley had finished taking everyone's orders, she'd returned to her spot at the table and sent Laney on her way. She hadn't realized that Laney was waiting for Paul, and Laney hadn't felt like giving her that information. So she'd just come downstairs to wait for him, selecting the first classroom as she came down the stairs for their meeting place.

"There wasn't anywhere else to sit," Laney said, gesturing to the child-sized desks that filled the room.

Paul joined her on the floor. "Here," he said, handing her a paper-wrapped sandwich half. "We had some leftovers."

"Thanks." She pulled a corner of the paper back to peek at the sandwich inside. Peanut butter-and-jelly.

"If I remember correctly, you prefer sandwiches off the kiddie menu."

Laney clenched her teeth. "You remember correctly." As he laughed, she added, "I don't like lunch meat, okay?"

"You're too much fun to tease," he said.

She took a grumpy bite of her sandwich. "Anyway, what did you want to tell me?"

He unwrapped his own food, taking a bite as well. "I had a mate of mine up in Seattle run a background check on your staff and volunteers. No criminal records."

"I could have told you that. We run background checks ourselves. Plus, this is a small town. We know everything about everyone who works for us."

Paul frowned. "Well, that's unfortunate."

"Why?"

"Because it makes narrowing down our suspect list more difficult. Someone with past experience of larceny would be an obvious jumping-off point. This leaves us back where we started."

"So, if the thief is someone who works for the museum, this is their first crime?"

"Or else they've never gotten caught." Paul took another bite of his sandwich. "Which will make it all the harder to catch them now. You might have to accept what that deputy told you yesterday, Laney—we may never find out what really happened to those paintings."

Laney looked down at her feet on the old, worn carpet. "We'll find them, Paul. I have faith in you." She gave him a sidelong glance. He was staring at her in surprise. "After all, you were the best investigative journalist on uView."

Paul snorted. "That's a pretty low bar. And I'm rusty now."

Laney's head quirked. "I'd think you'd be sharper than ever, working for a national cable news company."

Paul shook his head. "I'm a field reporter, Laney. The network isn't letting me run investigations."

She blinked in surprise. "They're not?" She hadn't realized— of course, she'd spent the last five years avoiding all news about Paul as much as she could.

"Nope. They said I'm too green."

"But that was why they *hired* you!" Laney protested. "You'd been doing it on uView for years! All those people who kept coming up to you when we—" She swallowed. "That is, you had millions of subscribers."

"Only about seven million. That's not that many," Paul said.

Laney scoffed. "Seven *million*'s not that many?"

"Not for uView. That Swedish uVer has a hundred million." When Laney gaped, he laughed. "Should have reviewed memes. It would have panned out better for me in the long run."

"You can't mean that," Laney said. "Becoming a journalist was your dream."

Paul smirked wryly, crumpling the paper his sandwich had been wrapped in into a ball. "It was, wasn't it? Be careful what you wish for, I suppose." He tossed the wrapper at the trash can next to the door. It bounced off the side.

"Do you regret it?" Laney asked.

"I don't know. Sometimes, I suppose. Sometimes I miss being independent." He stood up, going over to pick up the crumpled paper and tossing it into the trash can. "I thought I was doing the safe thing. I felt like it would be foolish to leave my livelihood reliant on a platform that demonetizes creators on a whim— particularly if they discuss politics, or anything else that could be deemed controversial."

"You were never afraid of controversy," Laney said with a smile.

"No," he replied, smiling back. Then he sighed. "I've gotten quite a bit of guff from the uVer community for taking a job with the legacy media. They think I'm a sellout."

She watched him thoughtfully. "You had to do what's right for you," she said.

He moved away from the door, going over to the frosted window and leaning against the sill. "The truth is, it's not all that reliable here, either. I still have to watch what I say. The network doesn't want me to make waves with the sponsors. When they first hired me, it made sense. I had a relatively big following, but I also had controversy from some of the investigations I'd done. They told me that the leash they were putting me on was temporary. That I just needed to prove to the investors and advertisers that I wouldn't mire the network in any sort of scandal. That once I'd proved myself, once I'd become a trusted name at the network, they'd give me more freedom. But it's been three years now, and I'm still not allowed to report on what I want. They're still sending me out on lightweight assignments."

"Like the one on the museum?" Laney asked dryly.

Paul looked at her intently. "No. I wanted that one," he said.

Laney's cheeks grew hot. "Why on earth would you want that one?"

He held her eyes. "I promised not to talk about it."

Laney's face was on fire, and she knew he had to see it. She didn't know how to respond, but fortunately, Paul's phone chimed loudly just then. He sighed, withdrawing it from his pocket. "Time to film the afternoon update. But look, I may have some other ideas about the investigation into the art theft. Would you be willing to meet up with me after we're done filming? We're going downtown. I'll just be a block or two away from the shop. I can meet you back there when I'm done?"

Laney hesitated, then nodded. "Sure," she said.

"Brill. I'll see you in about an hour."

A little over an hour later, Laney sat at her sewing desk behind the counter of the shop, organizing her thread by color. She probably should have been using this time to get caught up on her backlog, but she was too stressed out. Sewing the bedding had used up her ability to radiate calm for the day. It was important for her customers' sake that she not work while she was feeling this way, lest she inadvertently project her feelings into the seams. The last thing she needed was someone else ending up with a broken leg—or worse.

"Maybe if I let it pile up enough, the household fae will take pity on me and pitch in, like in 'The Shoemaker and the Elves,'" she said to herself, closing one drawer of thread and opening another. She'd never noticed any fae in the shop, though. Or in any other buildings in Foreston, for that matter. Outdoors, sure; they were all over town. But the only building they seemed willing to go inside was the Paine Mansion. Maybe because of the presence of the warren in the woods on the property? Grams had said something about that—something about the relationship of the warren's caretakers and the fae—but Laney couldn't remember it all now.

She sighed, closing the drawer and looking over the shop, past the glass front and across the street. People had been flocking in and out of Friedman's all day, most laden with N95 masks. Mr. Friedman had hung a sign in the window that said *Limit one box per customer*, but people had still been coming in droves. She'd even seen Suze about ten minutes ago, tucking a reusable shopping bag emblazoned with the logo of the Portland Art Museum into the trunk of her black Lexus.

That had given Laney a thought: The Portland Art Museum. Diane and her husband were members of the board there. Whoever had swapped out those paintings must have had a partner, someone who was a good enough artist that they could create such high-quality replicas. Someone on the board at an art museum would be bound to have artist connections, right?

And Diane had tried to stop Laney and Suze from calling the sheriff. Suze had said that was just Diane being contradictory as always, but what if she was wrong? What if Diane had another reason—like wanting to cover something up?

As Laney opened another thread drawer, the door to the shop opened with a jingling of bells. Laney glanced up to make sure it wasn't a customer pressing their luck despite the *Sorry, We're Closed!* sign in the window, but it was just Paul.

"Hey," she said, pushing the drawer shut again.

"You working?" Paul asked, coming over to the counter.

"Not really." Truthfully, she was just hiding from Carmen and Claudia. She'd heard their voices coming from her apartment when she got home, and she was sure that if she went up there, they'd manage to get the truth out of her about whether Paul had slept on the floor. It wouldn't matter to Claudia that a wall of pillows had been between them the whole night (well, most of it, anyway). She'd never let Laney hear the end of it.

She left the sewing desk and pulled up the hinged end of the countertop, gesturing for Paul to come back into the workspace. There were two tall stools behind the counter, and she motioned for him to sit at one while she took the other.

"What's the latest?" Laney asked as he leaned back against the counter.

"Twelve percent contained."

"Is that good or bad?"

"It's good, as long as they can keep it that way. Everyone's worried about the fact that the wind is supposed to pick back up tomorrow night. Even if this fire doesn't spread, a second one could start." Laney frowned, and Paul put his hand on her knee. "Try not to worry about it, okay? Everyone's doing the best they can."

Laney nodded, still frowning.

"Anyway, I've been giving this whole painting conundrum some thought," Paul said. "The insurance paperwork may have been stolen out of the office, but there must be copies somewhere, right? Do you have a scanned version somewhere?"

"I don't think so. Our record-keeping is still in the Stone Age. There was some talk of digitizing it, but I don't think it ever happened. Suze would know for sure." She let out a noise of frustration. "I just saw her, too. She was coming out of Friedman's. I wish I'd thought to stop her."

"No matter. What about the insurance agent? Surely they must have a copy."

Laney's eyes widened. "Of course! I know the woman who handles the insurance for the museum. Gladys Winthrop. Her agency is in The Dalles, but she has a home office behind her house. She calls it her 'She Shed.'"

Paul smirked. "Charming. Do you know how to get in touch with her?"

Laney nodded. "She's a friend of my mom's. I'm sure Mom must have her phone number." She hopped off the stool, going over to the sewing desk where she'd left her cell phone. "Hopefully she's still here. If she's evacuated, we might have to wait."

"And we know how you feel about that," Paul commented.

Laney quirked her eyebrow. "What's that supposed to mean?"

Paul chuckled and was about to respond when a noise in the distance made them both start.

Laney's stomach twisted. "Was that a siren?" she asked, though she knew—and dreaded—the answer.

Paul jumped off the stool and strode over to the window. Laney hurried after him, and a moment later, a bright red fire engine streaked past the shop.

"Fire?" Laney whispered. The siren was fading into the distance, but her ears were ringing. Not here, not now. Not so soon! Paul had just said the fire was more contained than it had been this morning... it couldn't have spread so fast...

Paul pulled out his phone, tapping a rapid-fire message to someone—probably someone on his crew. "You stay here, I'll go check it out," he said to Laney, shoving his phone back into his pocket.

"Are you kidding me? Absolutely not!" She grabbed her purse, rummaging through it and pulling out a mask and her keys.

"Laney, it is far too dangerous. You need to stay here and wait for evacuation orders if it's—"

"Paul," Laney said firmly, and he sighed.

"There's no talking you out of it. Of course not. Come on, then."

Chapter 14

Paul craned his head as they ran out of the shop. "The sirens still sound close. I'm going to guess that that's where they're heading." He pointed to a pillar of black smoke rising over the top of the row of historic storefronts that made up Main Street.

Laney looked up from unlocking her car and an acidic taste crept into her mouth. "So close?" If the wildfire had made it into town, there'd be no hope to save anything; not her store, not the museum... Foreston would be decimated.

"That doesn't look or smell like the wildfire smoke," Paul said reassuringly. "This is something else."

"Come on, then," Laney said, sliding into the driver's seat and turning on the ignition. Paul jumped into the passenger's side, and she quickly backed out of her parking spot in the alley beside the shop and headed in the direction they'd seen the fire engines go.

"Turn left at this stop sign," Paul said.

They found the source of the pillar of smoke just a few blocks away from downtown, in a historic neighborhood of 1920s Craftsman homes. As she looked for a place to park, her stomach began to sour again. The black smoke was rising from a dark blue house with white trim.

"A house fire?" Paul said as she pulled alongside the curb across the street and several houses down.

Laney swallowed hard, shutting the car off. "I know this house. This is where Gladys Winthrop lives."

Paul's eyebrows rose. "The insurance agent? The one you just told me about?"

"The very same."

She flung open her door and jolted at the cacophony that greeted her. There was the sound of shouting and the blast of water; the siren had been shut off, but the engine was still on, rumbling loudly enough to make the pavement beneath her feet vibrate. A crowd of neighbors was forming on the sidewalk, murmuring to each other as they watched the firefighters run back and forth from their truck into the backyard of the Craftsman, where the source of the smoke appeared to be.

But louder than all of that was the shrieking from the trees over Laney's head. It sounded like the screaming of a foreign tropical bird, or like the call of an eagle just before it swoops down on its prey. Less like the chatter of squirrels and more like the howl of a monkey.

It sounded nothing like it usually did, but Laney knew instinctively what it was.

Fae.

"Do you hear that?" she asked Paul as he slammed his car door.

"Some rather angry birds?" he theorized.

She shook her head, looking up. She could barely make them out; just a blur of movement, a streak of colors. But she could clearly see the branches of the trees overhead swaying in agitation. They were not pleased about the proximity of this fire to their home. And yet they weren't leaving. Laney bit her lip. Was Taryn right? Was it true that they *couldn't* leave?

She hurried to catch up with Paul, who was pushing past the crowd of neighbors on the sidewalk to get a better look at the fire situation. A woman in her late sixties stood near a wisteria-covered arbor to the side of the house, talking to one of the firefighters. A cobblestone path led from under the arbor into an unfenced backyard, where the blackened frame of a small outbuilding stood smoldering. Three other firefighters were blasting the smoking remains with water.

"Mrs. Winthrop," Laney said, hurrying over to the woman. "Are you okay?"

"Oh, Laney," the woman cried. On an ordinary day, Gladys Winthrop had a pixie-like face, with a perky upturned nose and thinly-plucked eyebrows that gave her a perpetually mischievous appearance. But there was no mischief to her now. She looked crushed.

"What happened here?" Paul asked, looking from the smoldering outbuilding to the firefighter.

"My She Shed!" Gladys wailed before the man got a chance to speak. "I was just taking my afternoon lie-down when I heard the alarm out back. By the time I made it downstairs, the whole thing was engulfed in flames!"

Paul shot Laney a wide-eyed look. He was thinking the same thing as her. Turning back to the firefighter, he asked, "Could this have been caused by an ember from the wildfire?"

"I'm sure that's what the culprit was hoping we'd think, but the fire is way too far off for that—especially now that the winds have died down. No, what we've got here is a sloppy arsonist without any regard for the rest of the community. We're dealing with a dangerous wildfire less than twenty miles out of town. We don't have the resources to deal with two fires at once. They're lucky this didn't get out of hand."

Laney sucked in a breath and then choked. The smoke from the wildfire was bad enough, but mingling with the smoke from the new fire made it a thousand times worse. "It was arson?" she asked between coughs.

"They found turpentine on the grass, Laney," Gladys said tearfully. "Turpentine! I can't believe anyone would want to hurt my poor little She Shed. Anyone besides *Frank*, anyway. And I can't exactly pin this on him."

"That outbuilding is where you keep your files, isn't it?" Paul asked.

Gladys nodded, and the firefighter said, "With that much paper inside, it was no wonder it went up like a Roman candle. The paint thinner may have gotten it started, but once the blaze was going it didn't need a whole lot of help. My guess is that someone around here has a lapsed fire insurance policy—probably someone who has experienced or is expecting property damage—and they wanted to eliminate the paper trail."

Just then, one of the other firefighters called to the man. He nodded and turned back to Gladys. "Excuse me, ma'am," he said, detaching himself from the group.

As Gladys stared at the husk of her former She Shed, Paul leaned over to Laney. "You know who else might want to eliminate the paper trail?" he whispered in her ear.

She nodded. "Whoever took the paintings."

Laney and Paul promised to stay with Mrs. Winthrop until a deputy arrived to make a report. She served them tea (Tetley, which Paul appreciated) out of a mismatched polka-dot tea set while regaling them with stories about her late husband, Frank, who'd hated the She Shed and had longed—loud and often—for its demise.

"If he were still with us, I'd suspect him of being the arsonist himself," she said, wiping a tear from her eye and glowering at a photo of her husband on the end table beside Laney. Laney glanced at the picture. If she didn't know better, she could have sworn there was a twinkle in the photograph's eye every time Gladys mentioned the She Shed's destruction.

A dozen neighbors filtered in and out while they waited, all eager to offer their condolences on the loss of Gladys's She Shed and to ask her, with thinly veiled excitement, if she had any idea who the culprit may have been. Everyone seemed eager to take their mind off the fire outside of town by focusing on the one right across the street.

By the time the deputy arrived, Laney had just about given up all hope of him ever showing up at all. It was near sunset when the doorbell rang, revealing the same deputy who had come by the museum to take Laney's report.

"You," he said when Laney answered the door. "Ms. McCarthy, isn't it? What are you doing here?"

"Mrs. Winthrop is a family friend," she explained. She glanced over her shoulder to where Gladys was once again crying to Paul over her Tetley about spiteful old Frank and his hatred of the She Shed. "And I'm also a bit concerned that this arson may have had something to do with the thefts at the museum." In a low voice, she told the deputy about how they'd discovered the insurance paperwork at the museum was missing, and Paul's theory that the thief may be trying to cover a paper trail to conceal any other missing paintings.

The deputy scribbled a few notes into a spiral-bound pad. "Right. And why didn't you call me when you noticed the missing paperwork?"

Laney ducked her head sheepishly. "We thought that it could have been misfiled," she said, omitting the part about herself and Paul doing some probing into the case themselves. He probably wouldn't take too kindly to that admission, even if he did acknowledge the fact that the department didn't have time to do any investigating of their own at the time being. "We didn't want to bother you until we were sure. But then when this fire happened..."

The deputy nodded with a *hmm*. "Well, it's certainly something to take into consideration. Thank you for the update," he said. "I'll look into this when I get the chance. Like I told you before, our resources are stretched pretty thin right now. Let me know if you find anything else missing from the museum."

Laney agreed, and the deputy went into the living room to take Mrs. Winthrop's report. Paul gratefully detached himself, and after the two of them once again gave Gladys their condolences on her She Shed, they pulled on their masks and left.

"She is a very... *interesting* lady," Paul said as they came down the front steps onto a cobblestone walkway.

"Yeah, she is. She's one of my mom's best friends," said Laney.

"Your mum must be very interesting as well," Paul remarked. "I'd love to meet her sometime."

Laney was unsure of how to respond. She remembered how Nancy had said, *"We never got a chance to meet him when you were in England."* Paul had always expressed interest in meeting her family back when they were dating, but after everything that had happened... the way she'd all but fled London after the term ended...

As she stood there, tongue-tied, a glimmer of color from the weeping cherry in the corner of Gladys's yard caught her eye. It flitted to and fro frantically, as if trying to get her attention. She stared for a moment, expecting it would disappear once her eyes came into focus, but it didn't vanish. It was definitely there, and definitely signaling to her.

A fae.

"Look," she said, jogging across the lawn to the tree and squinting to try to see it better. But even up close, she couldn't see more than a blurry wing and the snatch of a long, narrow face.

"I don't see anything," Paul said. Then, a moment later, it dawned on him. "You mean... one of *them?* Right here?"

Laney nodded. "What are you doing here?" she murmured as

the faery perched on the branch in front of her. It was harder to see when it wasn't moving, as the glow of color dimmed with its stillness. But it was definitely still there. "Don't you know it's not safe here?" She glanced at Paul. "That's what the noise was earlier. The 'angry birds.'"

"Was it?" Paul's eyebrow rose with interest. "Is it normal that I was able to hear them? I don't reckon that I have the Sight. I don't see anything right now, after all."

"Sometimes ordinary people can hear them. Especially if they're agitated the way they were earlier." She pursed her lips. "I don't like it, though. Taryn thinks..." She exhaled wistfully. "Taryn thinks they might not be able to leave. That they're bound to this place. To the warren at the Paine Estate. And if that's the case..."

Paul's eyes narrowed over his mask. "You have reason to be concerned about the wildfire spreading, then."

Laney nodded, glancing back at the blurry fae on the branch in front of her. "This faery had to have seen who set this fire. And I know the brownies saw who took the paintings. That's why they were trying to get my attention. But they can't tell me. It's so frustrating."

"Didn't you say your sister can see them better? Could she ask them?"

She shook her head. "She can see them, but she can't talk to them. I don't think anybody can. They speak a different language."

He made a thoughtful noise. "Does Taryn have a... a *gift* like you do? A 'faery blessing'?"

"Yeah," Laney said. "Psychometry. When she touches objects, sometimes she can see their past." Her eyes widened as a thought occurred to her. She looked up at Paul, who seemed to be having the same thought as her.

"The forged paintings—the thief must have spent a lot of time on them, right?" he asked.

"Exactly. It would have taken them days if not weeks to recreate those paintings as accurately as they did," she said eagerly.

"Which means that if Taryn touches the paintings..."

"...she might be able to see who the thief was. Come on." She hurried through Mrs. Winthrop's front gate, pausing on the sidewalk to glance at Paul. "Taryn's off tonight. I'll have her meet us at the museum. Maybe the fae can help us solve this mystery after all."

Chapter 15

It was almost nightfall as Laney turned onto Paine Parkway, the long, wooded avenue leading up the hill to the museum. The streetlights glowed an eerie orange in the smoky brown sky. Usually the drive onto the museum property was so peaceful and picturesque, especially on a summer evening. Laney bit her lip, wondering if she would ever see that view again. *Please,* she thought, *don't let the fire reach here. Keep this place safe.*

"There's someone coming from the museum," Paul remarked, pointing to a car approaching on the opposite side of the road.

Laney strained to make out the vehicle attached to the oncoming headlights. "Oh, it's Suze," she said, recognizing the black Lexus. "She must have come in this afternoon."

Suze stopped as Laney's car drew near, and Laney stopped as well, rolling down her window.

"You two heading to the museum?" Suze asked.

"Yeah, I... realized I left my wallet here yesterday," Laney lied. Even though Suze knew that Paul was helping her investigate the theft of the paintings, she felt weird about telling her the real reason they were heading to the museum now. She knew Suze didn't believe in the fae, and if she told her that they were working on the case, Suze might want to go back to the house with them. She didn't want Suze to see Taryn attempt to use her psychometry and decide that Laney was a fruitcake.

"You might need that," Suze replied, winking cheerfully. Then she frowned. "Did you hear about poor Mrs. Winthrop?"

"I did. She's a friend of my mother's," Laney explained.

"I feel awful. I know how attached she was to her She Shed," Suze said. "I had been planning on calling her on Monday to see if I could get copies of our paperwork from her. That's why I was here, digging through the file cabinet to make sure that we definitely didn't miss them."

"Any luck?" Laney asked.

"No. They may really be gone for good." Suze sighed. "And that's going to make claiming on our policy that much harder."

Laney winced. "I hope the papers wind up turning up somewhere in the office, then."

"Me too. Don't forget to alarm the house when you leave, okay?"

Laney agreed, and Suze rolled up her window, waving before driving away.

"She drives rather a nice car for an archivist at such a small museum," Paul commented when she'd gone, looking over his shoulder to watch the Lexus disappear down the hill. "I can't imagine she makes all that much at this job."

"Oh, no, definitely not," said Laney. "None of the staff here makes more than a few bucks over minimum wage. They're all hourly, too."

"Rich husband?"

Laney shook her head. "Suze isn't married. I think her family had money, though. As far as I know, only her sister is still living. But she must have gotten a big inheritance, because she lives in an even nicer house than Carmen and Josh do." She pulled through the wrought-iron gate at the end of the lane and onto the Paine mansion's narrow driveway. As she did, a light from the woods caught her eye. For a moment she thought it was just the reflection of her headlights, but then she saw it again and groaned.

"Something wrong?" Paul asked.

"I think we've got someone camping in the woods," she said.

"Does that happen a lot?"

"It's probably Bob. We usually turn a blind eye to him since he doesn't make too much of a mess, but I told him I didn't want him camping out here during the fire. It's too dangerous, especially with all this smoke." She sighed. "He needs to go to the Bible Fellowship. Let me get you into the house and I'll go tell him."

"I can come with you," Paul offered.

"No, no," Laney said. "Bob is a bit of an acquired taste, and he's worse with strangers around. I'm used to handling him. It's no problem."

Laney unlocked the front door of the house and turned off the alarm. "Taryn should be here any time," she told Paul as he stepped inside. "I'll be right back."

She went back out of the house toward the sloping trail leading to what the Paine family had called the "Secret Garden." Between the shadowed trunks of the trees around her, she could see the light of a lantern, bobbing slightly, as if the person holding it was moving around.

She pulled out her cell phone, swiping to turn on the flashlight app. She knew the trails around the museum like the back of her hand, but she hadn't traversed them often in the dark. The last thing she needed was to trip over a root or stumble on a rock. She walked carefully, looking back and forth frequently between the ground at her feet and the lantern ahead of her. The woods deepened around her until she turned and found she couldn't see the house anymore. Hadn't the lantern looked like it was pretty close to the road? It seemed like she'd been walking for a while, but that must have been a figment of her imagination—the clock on her phone said only a minute had passed, and she hadn't yet emerged into the Secret Garden. The trees around her looked unfamiliar, but then again, it was pretty dark in the woods.

She came around a bend in the trail, and suddenly the light on her phone flickered out. Her whole phone, in fact, went dead. She pressed the power button repeatedly, but it was unresponsive. How could the battery have died so quickly? She'd had 80% power just a minute ago. She stared down at the phone in her hand, then glanced over her shoulder at the trail behind her. Should she go back? She didn't love the idea of returning to the house in the dark, though. And she still needed to talk to Bob, try to get him to go to the Bible Fellowship. The light in front of her was still glowing bright. It looked like there might be a clearing just ahead. That's probably where he was camping.

She cautiously continued down the path, following the light. The leaves on the trees around her rustled, and above her an owl hooted, sounding strange and unfamiliar. It was answered with the whistle of a nightingale, and the scurrying of paws up the trunk to her right. As Laney reached the end of the trail, she saw that the lantern was not the only light illuminating the clearing. All around, tiny lights twinkled, like Christmas lights, but more delicate somehow. Smaller and in pastel colors, like those battery-operated strands Taryn had decorating her dorm room.

In the center of the clearing stood a weathered canvas tent in a faded green color. The front flap of the tent was unzipped, revealing a cot, a large camping pack, and a battery-operated hot plate. On a fallen log to the side of the tent, Bob sat, eating what looked like beans out of a worn saucepan. The lantern was on the ground at his feet.

"I figured it was you," Laney said as she entered the clearing.

"I figured it was you, too," Bob muttered in his gravelly voice.

"You're not supposed to be here, Bob."

"I'm always here. You've never said anything about it before."

Laney sighed. "I don't mind, ordinarily. But it's too dangerous out here now. Even if the fire never spreads this far, the smoke could make you really sick."

"No smoke in these woods," Bob replied.

"What?"

Bob pointed up, and Laney's eyes followed. Above her head, a small circle of sky peeked through the soaring tree canopy, dark purple and starry. A stark contrast to the brown sky she'd seen as she'd been driving.

Confused, Laney hesitantly removed her mask and inhaled through her nose. The air smelled clean, without a whiff of smoke.

"No smoke in these woods," Laney repeated quietly.

Bob took another bite of beans.

She watched him quizzically. "Bob," she said after a minute, "do you believe in the legend about there being faeries in Paine

Woods?"

"'Course. Any true Forestonian does." While Laney considered this, he added, "She was seen, you know."

Laney blinked in confusion. "Who was seen?"

"Woman who set that shed on fire."

Laney's jaw dropped. She stared at him, flabbergasted, as he took another bite of beans. "Who saw?" she demanded once he'd swallowed. "You?"

Bob merely grunted.

"Well, who was it? The arsonist, I mean. Did you recognize her?" she pressed.

He was quiet for a moment, his head quirked to one side. Laney was unsure whether he was thinking about it or just having one of his episodes. Somewhere behind his log, a lone cricket chirruped noisily.

"Bob, this is important!" Laney said in exasperation.

The old man narrowed his eyes at her. "Your trouble is that you're too doggone stubborn," he said. "Stubbornness blinds you, you know. Keeps you from seeing what's really in front of you. You get too set in your ways, you could lose what sight you do have."

Laney put her hands on her hips. "I don't have time for your riddles tonight, Bob. Someone's been stealing from the Paine Estate. Whoever set that shed on fire is almost certainly also the thief. So could you *please* just tell me who you saw?"

Bob sighed and shook his head. "It was one of them women who works at the museum."

Laney's eyes widened. That meant Paul's theory about the thief being a museum employee—or volunteer, possibly—was correct. And that whoever burned down Mrs. Winthrop's She Shed was also the thief.

"Which one, Bob? Could you describe her?"

He shrugged.

"Was she older? Blond hair, super tall?"

He shrugged again, pointedly. "All I can tell you is that it's one of the women who works at the museum."

That didn't narrow it down much—all the museum staff and most of the volunteers were women. But there was one woman in particular who had acted very suspiciously after Laney had told her about the theft of the paintings. And that same woman had connections to the art world. There was only one person it could be.

"Okay. Thanks, Bob," she said. "You've been... a lot of help." As much help as could be expected from Crazy Old Bob, anyway. "You can stay for tonight, but I want you to be really careful, all right? Pay attention to if it starts smelling smoky. And if the sheriff gives an evacuation order, you have to leave."

"Whatever you say," he muttered.

"I'm serious, Bob!"

"Yes, ma'am." He glared at her before taking another bite of beans.

Satisfied, Laney turned to leave the clearing. She wasn't sure how she was going to make it back to the house in the dark, but just a few steps out of the clearing, her phone flickered back to life. Sighing with relief, she hurried back up the path toward the house. The smell of smoke soon returned to her nose, and she pulled her mask back up over her face, glancing over her shoulder in the direction of Bob's campsite.

The light from the lantern had disappeared between the trees.

Chapter 16

The walk back up to the house seemed to take less time than it had to reach Bob's campsite. According to her phone, she'd only been gone for five minutes, though it had felt more like an hour. She still couldn't believe what Bob had told her. That he'd actually *seen* the arsonist. That meant their theory had to be correct. Someone from the museum had stolen the paintings. Now they just had to find the proof.

Hopefully, Taryn would be able to give them that.

As she opened the front door of the museum, she found that Taryn had already arrived. The sound of her laughter echoed off the high ceiling of the entryway. Laney winced as she realized that she'd left Paul and her sister unsupervised—she'd been so preoccupied by the sight of Bob's lantern in the woods, she hadn't considered the tactical error of letting the two of them meet without Laney there to kick Taryn in the shins if she veered into unapproved discussion territory.

Please may he not have told her where he's staying, she thought desperately. *Please please please please—*

"Ah, Laney," Paul said, noticing her standing in the doorway. "I was just getting to know your charming sister."

Taryn turned to face Laney, an irascible grin on her face. "D'you hear that, Laney? I'm charming."

"You're a turd," Laney grumbled, closing the front door and locking the deadbolt.

"A *turd*? Who are you, Matthew?"

"Could you be a little louder? I'm not sure if they can hear you down at the Brownstone. Are you *trying* to broadcast that we're here to all of Foreston?" Laney said, ignoring Taryn's comment. Maybe she *had* sounded a little like their older brother there. But that didn't mean it was wrong.

Taryn rolled her eyes. "Why did you call me out here, anyway? For some kind of secret spy mission?"

"You're not too far off the mark," Paul said. "What has Laney told you about the art thefts here at the museum?"

Taryn's eyebrows shot all the way up her forehead. "Um, absolutely *nothing*?" She glared at Laney. "You think you might have mentioned something like that."

"There's been a lot going on, okay?" Laney protested. "I would have told you that night at the Brownstone, but you were too busy sticking your nose where it doesn't belong, so I didn't get a chance to get a word in edgewise. And then the fire started, and..." Laney sighed. *And everything else that you are* also *supposed to know nothing about.* "Never mind."

She quickly gave Taryn a rundown of everything that she'd discovered since Friday, the digging she and Paul had been doing, and finished it off with the arson of Mrs. Winthrop's She Shed this afternoon.

"Wow," Taryn said, letting out a shaky breath. "That's... wow. A lot." She looked at Laney quizzically. "But I don't understand why you called me out here. I don't see how I can help."

"Well"—Laney shifted awkwardly—"Paul and I were talking. About, you know, how the brownies attracted my attention to the swapped painting. And then there was another fae this afternoon, at Gladys's house. And I said it was too bad that we couldn't just ask them, and then Paul suggested that maybe your faery blessing might help."

Taryn arched a brow. "You told him about our faery blessings?"

"I mean, he technically already knew. From... before. You know, in college."

"Ah." Taryn looked between Laney and Paul, a sly grin spreading across her face. "I see. So you think that my psychometry can help?"

"Right," said Paul, jumping in quickly when he noticed Laney's crimson face. "You can see objects' history, right? So if you touch the paintings, maybe you can see the thief."

"Maybe." Taryn frowned. "But I can't exactly control it on command. Every once in a while, I get a vision right away, but a lot of times it doesn't come until later. Like when I'm asleep, I'll dream it. But more often I don't get anything at all."

Paul nodded thoughtfully. "Right. I can imagine it wouldn't happen for everything; otherwise, you wouldn't be able to touch anything at all."

"Exactly."

"But it's still worth a try, isn't it?" Paul went on. "Maybe you won't get anything. But maybe you will."

Taryn sighed. "I suppose you're right." She shot Laney a glance. "Mom and Dad aren't going to be happy about you getting involved in this instead of leaving it to the sheriff, though."

Laney crossed her arms. "Then it's a good thing you're not going to tell them."

Taryn rolled her eyes again and nodded.

"How many paintings have been stolen, anyway?" Taryn asked as Laney led her into the parlor.

"Just the two that we know about," Laney replied. "There could be more, though. I had stared at this one enough from sewing that dress for the auction that I recognized the difference. But I might never have even noticed it without the fae. I definitely wouldn't have caught the other one on my own. And with our paperwork missing, and Mrs. Winthrop's She Shed burned down, unless the fae attract my attention again, I may never notice if there are more."

"There should be another set of insurance papers down at her main office, though, right?" Taryn pointed out.

"That's right," Paul said. "Didn't you say that the outbuilding in her garden was just a home office?"

"Yeah, her main office is in The Dalles," said Laney. "Hopefully those copies are safe—with the fire, we're kind of trapped here. If we leave town, they might not let us come back."

"Well, if we're trapped here, the thief is as well," Paul pointed out.

"Okay. I'll call them tomorrow morning and find out if they do have the papers on file," Laney said.

"So it's this painting?" Taryn asked, pointing to the portrait next to the dress form.

"Yes."

Taryn reached her hand out, hesitating. "You want me to just touch the painting? Won't that damage it?"

Laney rolled her eyes. "It's a forgery, Taryn. Who cares if you damage it?"

Taryn bit her lip and nodded, gingerly touching one corner of the painting with her fingertips. She closed her eyes. For a long moment, everything was quiet.

She exhaled and dropped her hand away from the painting. "Nothing. Sorry, guys."

"That's all right," Paul said. "Maybe it will come to you later."

"There's the other painting, too," Laney suggested. "The one in the hallway by the dining room. We could give it one more try."

"Okay," said Taryn.

Laney chewed on the inside of her cheek as she led them down the hall. She knew it was a long shot, but this was still their best chance at figuring out who the thief was. The fae knew something was wrong. They were the ones who had warned her in the first place, here and then again at Mrs. Winthrop's. They *knew* what was going on. They had to want Laney to know the truth. So why weren't they using Taryn's power to help them?

"Here it is," Laney said, stopping in front of the impressionist landscape.

"This is the one the fae alerted you to?"

"Yeah. There was a fork missing from our silverware set. I found it lying on the floor here, and then when I looked at the painting, I saw one of them. Right here." She put her hand on the ornate frame, gingerly. She closed her eyes for just a moment. *You have to show us who it was,* she thought, as if she were willing the painting to talk. *The only way we can help is if you show us. Please.*

"Look, Laney, there's one!"

Laney's eyes snapped open. "What?"

Taryn pointed. At first Laney didn't see anything; but then she noticed a bronze smudge of light peeking around the door of the dining room. "It's a brownie," Taryn said, crouching in front of it. "Hey, there," she said, reaching out her hand, one finger extended. It looked like she was trying to get a cat to approach her and sniff her fingers. But rather than sniff them, Laney could just make out the blurry silhouette reaching its own hand out to touch Taryn's.

Taryn giggled. "Nice to meet you," she said. "Are you the one who told my sister about that painting?"

The creature squeaked something incomprehensible back at her.

"I heard that," Paul said. "Sounds like a mouse."

"They do to the average ear, when you can hear them at all," Taryn said. Looking back at the brownie, Taryn murmured, "Would you help me? We're trying to find who did this."

Laney squinted to try to see the creature better. It was quiet for a moment, then she saw a glimmer of motion. The creature stepped into Taryn's hand, and Taryn lifted it to her shoulders.

"I think it's going to help me," Taryn said. "Let me give it a try." Closing her eyes, she reached out and touched the painting gingerly in the corner, as she had with the portrait. She was still for a minute, her eyes shut, holding her breath. The whole house went silent.

Impulsively, Laney reached her hand out, too, placing it back on the frame. "Help us," she whispered.

Beside her, Taryn gasped, jerking her hand away from the painting.

"Taryn!" Paul exclaimed. "Are you all right?"

Taryn swallowed. "I'm fine. I got something."

Laney could feel her pulse quicken. "You saw the thief?"

"I'm not sure. I think so. It was a woman. I recognized her, but I can't put my finger on it." She crouched, lowering the brownie from her shoulder. "Thank you," she whispered, smiling at the creature. "You were more help than you know."

"You recognized her?" Laney prodded once the blurred figure had scurried into the shadows. "Was she someone who works here at the museum? Did she have blonde hair?"

"You're still thinking it's Diane?" Paul asked.

"She's the most logical suspect," Laney pointed out. "And Bob said that the person who set the She Shed on fire was someone who works at the museum."

"I'm sorry, Crazy Old Bob *saw* the arsonist?" Taryn asked incredulously, straightening. "And you neglected to share that with us?"

"I didn't get a chance!" Laney protested. "You were too busy *charming* Paul when I got back."

"All right, all right," Paul said, stepping between the sisters. "That's unimportant. Taryn, was the person you saw just now someone who works at the museum?"

Taryn shook her head. "No. I'm not sure who it was. I swear I recognized her, but I can't think of how or why. It definitely wasn't Diane, though."

Laney groaned. "Great. Well, that brings us back to the drawing board, then."

"It's okay. It will come to her," Paul said.

Taryn nodded. "I'll keep thinking about it. Maybe it will be more clear after a good night's sleep."

Laney tried to keep her disappointment from showing on her face. The more time passed, the more likely it was that the culprit would get away. And if Taryn said that it wasn't someone from the museum, then that would make it all the harder to catch them.

Paul nudged her shoulder. "Let's call it a night and regroup in the morning. What do you say?"

"Yeah, why don't you guys come by the Penngrove for breakfast tomorrow?" Taryn suggested. "I'm working the morning shift. I can let you know if I got any other visions in the night."

"Sounds good," Paul said, pulling his phone out of his back pocket to check the time. "I'm due for the evening report now. Laney, could you give me a ride?"

Laney nodded, trying to ignore the sly glance that Taryn was giving her. "Okay," she said, "let me get the alarm set and we can get out of here."

Chapter 17

Laney trudged up the stairs to her apartment. After the day she'd had, she was exhausted. She wanted nothing more than to crawl into bed and sleep for eleven hours. But she could tell by the sound of animated chatter inside that Carmen and Claudia were still up and would undoubtedly pounce on her the moment she came in the door. She'd been able to avoid them earlier; now it was time to pay the piper.

"Hi, guys," she said as she opened the door.

"Oh, good, you're here just in time," Carmen said, gesturing to the coffee table in front of them. It was covered in white cardboard boxes with red Chinese writing on them. "We got dinner delivered. I got an order of lemon chicken just for you."

"Yum," Laney said, feeling her stomach rumble at the sight of the food. "Exactly what I need after a day like today."

"Been keeping busy?" Claudia asked, her mouth turning up impishly. "I heard a little rumor that you and a certain reporter were spotted around town a lot today. Helping out at the Bible Fellowship, for one thing."

Laney sighed, pulling a plastic fork out of the delivery bag and grabbing the little white carton with lemon chicken in it. "Word travels fast, doesn't it?"

"It does indeed," Carmen agreed.

"So," Claudia said, "how goes your renewed acquaintance with Mr. Nelson? From the time you've been spending together, I'd say that it hasn't been as bad as you expected."

"It's fine," Laney said. She took a bite of chicken and jumped as she felt a sharp poke in the side of her knee. She glanced down to see that Sofia had emerged from under the secretary desk and was looking at her expectantly. She pulled off a small piece of meat and handed it to the eager cat.

"Just fine, huh? And how did having him as a roommate last night work out?"

Laney rolled her eyes. "Also fine."

Carmen watched her quietly. Finally, she said, "You know, I haven't spent a lot of time with him, but Paul seems like a really good guy. He brought all that food for the people sheltering at the church. He gave up his hotel room. He probably would have given up his cot, too, if he'd made it over to the church and found they needed more beds."

Laney looked down at the floor. Sofia had finished chewing and stretched up again when she saw Laney looking in her direction, poking her eagerly for more chicken.

"Paul is a good guy," she said softly, breaking off another piece of meat for Sofia.

"So why were you so mad when you found out he was doing the story on the museum? What happened between you two in college?" When Laney opened her mouth to protest, Carmen interrupted, "I know you said you don't want to talk about it. But I think you *need* to, Laney. Whatever happened, you clearly haven't resolved it yet. And if you're going to move forward, you can't keep avoiding it."

"Nothing is going on between me and Paul," Laney said quickly, her face hot.

Claudia arched an eyebrow. "No one said anything was."

"I didn't mean move forward with *him*," Carmen said. "I meant move forward with your life." She hesitated. "Unless you *want* to move forward with him...?"

Laney sighed, pulling off another piece of chicken for Sofia while she attempted to collect her thoughts. "Okay," she said finally. Her tongue felt like lead. But still, she knew she needed to tell someone. After all this time... she needed to tell someone.

"Taryn told you that we dated in college." She swallowed. "I studied abroad in London my junior year, and Paul and I started dating a few months after I got there. We were in a writing class together."

"And that was when he was a uVer, right?" Claudia asked.

Laney nodded. "His channel really took off that year we were dating. He would get recognized when we went out sometimes. People would come up and want to get their pictures taken with him. Tourists especially. Sometimes it was guys who just wanted to chat about the political stories he was covering. But other times, it was girls." She frowned. "Toward the end, it was girls more often than guys."

"Because he's good-looking?" Claudia surmised. Carmen was watching silently, her expression thoughtful.

"Yeah. So I started reading the comments on his videos. He had, like... a *fanclub* of girls. They were drooling over him on every video. And some of them were acting... I don't know, almost like they knew him. Calling him by his first name instead of by his screen name, making in-jokes in the comments, stuff like that. Some of them even knew things about his family. I don't know if they really knew him or if they were just stalking him." She paused. "There was a fan Wiki about his channel that had a lot of that information on it."

"Well, did you talk to him about it?" Carmen spoke up at last.

Laney swallowed, watching Sofia sniff the chicken she'd just given her. Apparently, the cat was now bored with lemon chicken, because she left the piece uneaten and moved over to Carmen, who was eating barbecue pork.

She took a shaky breath and closed her eyes. "The weekend before I came back to the States, we were supposed to meet up at a pub near campus. Some of his friends from high school or whatever they call it in England were visiting and he wanted me to meet them. I had been doing stuff for the drama department, so by the time I got to the pub, there was already a big crowd inside. And when I came in, I saw him standing near the bar with a big group of people. Some were guys, but there were girls there, too. And this one girl... she had her arm around his neck, and right when I came in the door, they—"

She broke off, squeezing her eyes shut. That was the first time she'd spoken these words aloud, and they burned her tongue like acid. She tried to block the memory out of her mind, but it kept replaying, over and over.

Beside her, Carmen gasped. "Were they—kissing?" she whispered in horror.

"I—I'm not sure. A big guy bumped into me and yelled at me for blocking the door, and I just took off and went back to the halls." *Ran* back to the halls, actually, she remembered wryly. And then proceeded to cry her eyeballs out.

"What did he say when you asked him about it?" Carmen

wanted to know.

Laney hesitated.

"You *did* ask him about it, right?" Claudia said incredulously.

Laney opened her mouth to answer, but just then, the apartment door opened. She jumped, her heart leaping into her throat, and Sofia shot back under the secretary desk at the sudden movement.

"Good evening, ladies," Paul said, closing the door behind him. He looked back and forth between the three of them, hesitating. "Sorry, am I interrupting something?"

"No, no," Laney said quickly. "We were just having dinner. Did you eat yet? How do you feel about Chinese?"

"That sounds delicious," he replied, coming over to look at the array of cartons on the coffee table. Laney pulled her knees up into her chest, looking down at the floor again. Under the secretary desk, Sofia's tail twitched.

She could feel Carmen watching her, but she refused to meet her eyes.

Chapter 18

It was less smoky the next morning as she and Paul headed over to the Penngrove for breakfast. The air wasn't as stagnant now that the breeze had picked back up again. There had been no further progress at containment, but so far, the firebreaks had been holding. As long as the wind didn't get too strong, there was a chance the fire might not spread any farther.

That would be one piece of good news, at least.

"You're rather quiet this morning," Paul said as Laney turned into the hotel's parking lot.

"I'm just tired," Laney said. "This weekend was... a lot."

Paul nodded. "My trip to Foreston definitely hasn't gone as planned, that's for sure."

Laney glanced over at him. "In a bad way or a good way?"

The corner of his mouth quirked up impetuously. "You tell me."

She looked away from him, pulling into a spot and putting her car in park. While it wasn't untrue that this weekend's events had left her feeling more than a little frayed around the edges, the biggest reason for her fatigue today was the fact that she hadn't slept a wink last night. Her conversation with Carmen and Claudia had kept playing over and over in her head until her mind was raw. Neither of the sisters had said anything to her about it this morning, but it had been in their every pointed glance this morning as Laney helped them get their things packed up and Sofia inserted—hissing and squirming—back into her cushioned carrier. Josh was due to arrive at the airport this evening, and Carmen was eager to get there early in case there was traffic. With the highways closed, they'd have to go up through Yakima, adding a good two or three hours to their trip.

As she'd hugged Laney goodbye, Carmen had given her a meaningful look. "Keep me posted," she'd said. And though that seemed a perfectly normal thing to say considering the circumstances, Laney had gotten the distinct impression that there was more to it in this case.

"*You* did *ask him about it, right?*"

"Everything okay?"

Paul was watching her intently, but she didn't meet his eyes. "Fine," she mumbled, grabbing her purse and fumbling for the car door.

They bypassed the main hotel entrance, heading instead for

the east wing of the building, where the restaurant was located. As Paul pulled open the door for her, the hubbub of voices and the scent of fresh bacon and hot brewed coffee rushed out to greet her, strong enough to overpower the smokiness of outside. Laney felt herself relax a bit as she looked around the cozy interior. The walls of the restaurant were adorned with vibrant artwork and colorful swags of dried flowers. The big brick fireplace on the back wall stood empty, its glass shutters pulled closed for the summer and a large floral arrangement in a painted wooden crate set in front of it. The dining room was bright and cheery enough to make Laney's problems suddenly seem far away.

A server bustled past with a tray laden with pancakes, and Laney's stomach growled loudly enough to be heard over the noise of the crowd. Beside her, Paul laughed.

"Someone's hungry," he chuckled in her ear.

Laney jumped away from him as if she'd been burned. "Y-yeah," she stammered, avoiding his eyes. "Starving, actually. Hopefully we'll be able to get a table. I've never seen it so busy, especially on a weekday."

Paul didn't say anything in response. When she glanced back in his direction, he was studying her thoughtfully. He quickly covered it, but she noticed for just an instant that something in his eyes looked vulnerable, and maybe a little hurt. She felt a pang of guilt. It wasn't fair, the way she was acting. But that wasn't anything new, was it?

Before she could say anything to try to diffuse the awkwardness, Taryn bustled up to them. "Hey, guys," she said, sounding out of breath. "I hope you haven't been waiting long."

Laney shook her head. "No, we just got here."

"Great. As you can see, things are just a little hectic here. But no worries, I made sure to save you a table." Taryn gestured to the back corner of the restaurant, where a small round table stood empty save for a syrup caddy with a sign that read *Reserved* taped to the top of it.

Taryn grabbed a couple menus out of the host stand and motioned for them to follow her. Paul held back, sweeping his arm in front of him to indicate for Laney to go first, the expression on his face so normal that Laney wondered for a moment whether she'd imagined the look she'd seen in his eyes a moment ago.

But she knew she hadn't.

"I'll go grab you some waters," Taryn said as Laney and Paul took their seats. In spite of herself, Laney yawned as she turned to hook her purse on the back of her chair, and Taryn laughed. "Or should I make that coffee?"

"I think coffee sounds like a fantastic idea," Paul said with an easy grin. "I haven't been sleeping too well myself."

"Oh, yeah, I heard that you checked out of the hotel. Where have you been staying, Paul?" Taryn asked, and Laney's blood ran cold. She shot Paul a wild-eyed look that he didn't seem to notice.

"A good Samaritan loaned me their couch," Paul replied

without hesitation.

"Oh, that's nice. Forestonians are nothing if not neighborly. Who—" Taryn broke off, noticing that Laney had slumped down on the table, her hair fanned out around her in a messy puddle. "What's your problem?"

Laney lifted her head just enough to glare at Taryn through strands of copper hair. "I need coffee."

"All right, all right, I'll bring a pot over." Taryn glanced over her shoulder at the host stand, where a middle-aged couple was now standing, waiting to be seated. She let out a barely audible groan. "As soon as I take care of these people, that is."

"No rush," said Paul as Taryn bustled away. He turned back to face Laney, a smirk on his face. "Close one, eh? But that was a nice save on my part, if I do say so myself."

Laney pushed herself up on her elbows and looked down at her menu. A card poking out of the laminated folds read, *Today's specials: Crepes filled with Marionberries and sweet creme, dusted in powdered sugar; Strawberry Belgian waffles with whipped topping and our house-made lemon curd.*

"She didn't say anything about the thief," Laney commented, her eyes focused on the words on the specials card without taking any of them in.

Paul snorted. "Well, give her a minute. We just walked in the door."

"If she hasn't figured out who that woman is, then we might as well kiss those paintings goodbye." She flushed, instantly regretting the phrasing of that sentence.

"Just relax," Paul said soothingly. "You're not going to make any of this better by getting so worked up about it."

"Way too late for that," Laney muttered.

Paul was quiet for a long moment. She could feel his eyes staring at her again, but she refused to look up at him. Finally, he sighed. "All right, what did I do?" he asked.

She looked up at him in surprise. "You didn't do anything."

"Then why are you being this way?"

Her jaw worked soundlessly. Her first instinct was to deny that she was being any particular way, but she was getting sick of making up excuses, and she could tell that Paul was getting sick of hearing them. "I'm tired," she finally said.

"There's more to it than that."

"And I'm stressed out," she added.

"And?"

She gritted her teeth. "And we agreed that we weren't going to talk about it."

"I've decided that I don't like the terms of that agreement."

"You don't get to change your mind after you've agreed!" Laney protested.

"Well, I didn't really get a say about it, now, did I?" Paul's eyes sparked. "That's how it always is with you, isn't it? You decide something's going to be a certain way, and I just have to go along with it. My opinion doesn't matter. My feelings don't matter. Well, I'm not playing along anymore, Laney. I came here for a purpose, and I'm not leaving until I accomplish that purpose, even if it means I have to violate your royal decree."

Laney's stomach knotted as his eyes held hers. And what purpose was that, exactly?

Before she could respond, Taryn set a full pot of coffee down on the table with a *thunk*. "Sorry it took so long," she said. "Did anyone come to take your order?"

Laney jumped, her heart hammering in her throat. "Not yet," she said quickly.

Taryn sighed in a long-suffering way. "I have to do everything around here."

"We don't mind waiting," Paul said politely, though it was obvious from his tone and expression that he was more than slightly annoyed by Taryn's interruption.

"Have you had any luck figuring out who the person you saw in your vision was?" Laney asked.

Taryn shook her head. "No, and it's driving me insane. I was hoping I might see more in my dreams last night, but it was just a replay of that same vision I got in the house yesterday. I know I know who that woman is, but I just can't put my finger on it. Oh, hold on a minute." She looked up as the door from the restaurant into the main part of the hotel opened and a man in a khaki jumpsuit entered, followed by two younger men carrying a large rectangular package wrapped in brown paper. Taryn relaxed. "Sorry, I thought it was more guests coming in to be seated."

Laney watched as the maintenance men carried the package over to the fireplace and removed the paper, revealing a huge painting of a watermill beside a picturesque stream. Tall reeds grew in the foreground, painted in delicate brush strokes.

"Wasn't that painting on the fireplace before?" Laney asked, watching as the men maneuvered it into place over the mantel. "Why'd they take it down?"

"Oh, management was having it cleaned. It had some residue on it from the fireplace," Taryn said. "We had Suze's sister do it. She's an art restorer in Portland." Taryn froze, her eyes wide and her mouth in the shape of an O. "Laney!" she hissed at last. "That's who it was!"

Laney sucked in her breath. "What?"

Taryn nodded frantically. "Suze's sister! That's who I saw in the vision!"

Laney blinked repeatedly. "Are you *sure*?"

"Yes! I've only met her a couple times, but I know that's who it was. They had dinner here one night—Suze is the one who recommended her sister to my boss. She pointed out how dingy the painting had gotten and told us that her sister could touch it up for us. Her sister's name is... Seleste, that's right. I remember thinking it was weird because it's spelled with an S."

Laney put her head in her hands. The room felt like it was

spinning. Suze? *Suze* was the thief? It just couldn't be possible. There had to be some kind of mistake.

"I'm not wrong, Laney," Taryn said urgently. "You have to believe me. I *know* that's who it was."

Laney swallowed, looking up at her. "I know. I do believe you."

"It makes sense," Paul said thoughtfully. "Art restorers are often trained artists themselves. And they have to be good enough at imitating the original artist's style that their touch-ups won't be noticeable. Someone with that kind of skill, particularly if they're talented... they could probably make the best forgeries if they put their mind to it."

Laney nodded slowly. Paul had pointed it out himself yesterday—Suze led a very expensive lifestyle for someone with the kind of job she had. What if she wasn't just living on family money? Laney vaguely remembered Viv mentioning that Suze had worked at a dozen museums all over the country over the course of her career. Were any of those museums missing valuable paintings from their collections?

"It makes perfect sense. It's just... Suze. She's so... *nice.*"

Paul watched her for a moment. "Not as ideal a suspect as Diane, then?"

She sighed. "No. But that's not what matters. Catching the thief—no matter who it is—is the important thing. My feelings, my... bias... That's not what's important. The truth is." She swallowed, her face burning. "A very smart journalist once told me that."

She didn't want to look at him, but she could feel Paul watching her again. When she glanced up, she saw the corner of his mouth quirked up thoughtfully. "Right," he said, catching and holding her eyes.

"So we know who the thieves are. But what are we going to do about it?" Taryn asked. "It's not exactly like a psychometric vision brought on by faery intervention is going to hold up in a court of law."

Laney shook her head. "No. What we need is real evidence."

Paul sat back in his chair, folding his arms. "I'd say it's fair to assume Suze is the one who set Mrs. Winthrop's shed on fire yesterday. You said that Bob bloke saw who did it, right? Do you suppose he'd be willing to testify to that?"

"Hard to say." Laney chewed her lip thoughtfully. "It's not exactly easy to get a straight answer out of him. I'd prefer to leave that as a last resort."

"You said they'd found turpentine on the grass, right?" Taryn said. "Could that somehow be traced to Suze?"

"Doubtful. If her sister's an art restorer, she'd have easy access to the stuff," said Paul.

"Wait," Laney said, reaching out a hand to grab Taryn's shirtsleeve. "I saw her at Friedman's yesterday afternoon, probably no more than twenty minutes before the fire started."

"You don't think she'd be so stupid as to have bought the

turpentine there, though, do you?" Taryn said.

"Desperate people do desperate things," Paul said. "If our theory is right, it seems likely they've been doing this for a while. But this is the first time they've ever been close to being caught."

"The only way to know is to go talk to Mr. Friedman," Laney said, jumping to her feet.

"So sorry about the wait," said a teenage girl dressed, as Taryn was, in all black. She approached the table with a pad of paper in hand. "What can I get you?" She looked in confusion from Laney to Taryn to Paul, then back to Laney. "Sorry, did you still want to order?"

Laney was about to tell her to forget it, but Paul quickly said, "Yes, we do!" When Laney shot a look at him, he added, "We'll get it to go. But whatever it is we're doing today, I'm not facing it on an empty stomach."

Chapter 19

Half an hour later—after wolfing down their breakfast in the car on the way back from the Penngrove—Laney and Paul headed from the alley next to McCarthy's Magic Touch across the street to Friedman's Hardware. It was a small shop compared to the big box warehouse stores that Laney had seen in larger towns, but Mr. Friedman always managed to carry the most essential tools and supplies that the average person would need. And, of course, he was happy to place special orders for people who needed bigger ticket items like lumber or flooring.

A bell jangled overhead as Laney opened the door to the shop. Compared to the day before, the hardware store was surprisingly quiet. Just a few customers milled around, browsing paint chips and differently sized lag bolts.

Mr. Friedman didn't even look up from the register where he

was counting out change as the door swung closed behind Laney and Paul. He just called out, "All out of masks," and pointed vaguely at a sign on the counter beside him that read, *N95 respirators out of stock! New shipment expected Tuesday.*

"Oh, um, we weren't here for those," Laney said as she approached the counter.

Mr. Friedman looked up. "Oh, Laney! How can I help you?"

"We just had a couple questions for you," she said in a low voice, looking around the store surreptitiously. "If we could keep it confidential, that would be great."

Mr. Friedman looked at her like she'd lost her mind. "What're you on about?" he asked at a volume far too high for Laney's liking.

She winced, holding a finger to her lips. "Please, Mr. Friedman. This is really important."

The store owner narrowed his eyes at Paul, who had come up to the counter beside Laney. "This isn't for that news show, is it? Because I'm not a fan of his network. You wouldn't catch me watching cable news."

"Can't fault you for that, sir," Paul said. "They may pay my bills, but you wouldn't catch me watching them myself."

Mr. Friedman smirked, seeming pleased by that response.

"It's not for the news," Laney whispered. "It's about the museum."

"Usually Hank from the parks department orders the

maintenance supplies," Mr. Friedman said.

Laney shook her head. "Mr. Friedman, please. Just listen to me. Did you see Suze when she was here yesterday?"

"Who?"

Laney clenched her teeth. Since her parents had owned the store across the street her whole life, she'd known Mr. Friedman since she was a little girl. But just like all the other residents of Foreston, he had a way of driving her crazy. "The collections manager at the museum. Suzette Cherniske."

"Oh, *Suze*!" Mr. Friedman exclaimed. "Why didn't you say so?" Beside Laney, Paul's shoulders shook with silent laughter. "Now, you say she was here yesterday?"

"I saw her leave the store yesterday around two-thirty."

"Hmm, I don't remember. I think at least half the town was in here yesterday, buying masks."

"I don't think she bought masks," said Laney. "Or at least, that's not all she bought. She might have bought turpentine. Does that sound familiar?"

The man distractedly pulled a worn pencil out of the breast pocket of his flannel shirt and started chewing on the eraser. Laney winced.

"She may have bought turpentine. She's done it before."

Laney's eyebrows rose. "She has?"

Mr. Friedman nodded. "Sometimes she helps her sister out

with that art restoration business. Turpentine is a thinning medium for oil paints. 'Course, a lot of painters like to use mineral spirits instead. But Suze's sister, she likes turpentine."

"But you can't confirm whether she bought any yesterday?" Paul asked.

Mr. Friedman shook his head.

"Does your computer store records of your daily transactions?" Paul suggested.

Mr. Friedman snorted. "Don't have a computer. Just this." He gestured to the ancient cash register on the counter. Laney knew that it didn't even have a scanner for the items' barcodes. It was the kind where you had to enter the item price manually.

"Okay," she said. "Thanks anyway, Mr. Friedman. Could you do me a favor and not tell anyone that we spoke to you, or what we talked about?"

Mr. Friedman frowned. "You're sure this isn't for the news?"

"Yes!" Laney cried in exasperation. "Just *trust* me, okay?"

"Whatever you say," Mr. Friedman said, putting his chewed pencil back into his shirt pocket. Paul thanked the man for his time, and they left the store.

"So we're back to square one, then," Paul said, pulling on his mask and falling into step alongside Laney as she stormed across Main Street. "Suze very well may have purchased turpentine yesterday, but we've got no proof. And since she regularly buys it anyway, it would be difficult to provide enough probable cause in order for the sheriff to get a warrant to search her house."

"We need irrefutable evidence," Laney said. "We've got to prove beyond a shadow of a doubt that Suze is the one who torched Mrs. Winthrop's office, and that she stole the paintings." Laney paused on the sidewalk, looking up at the patch of yellow-gray sky over the roof of her store, where yesterday a plume of black smoke had billowed.

"What are you thinking?" Paul asked, eyeing her.

"I'm thinking about what Taryn said last night, about the main office having copies of our insurance paperwork." She pulled out her phone, glancing at the time. It was just after ten o'clock. "I think we need to set a trap."

A quick phone call to Gladys's main office in The Dalles had confirmed that the main office did indeed have copies of the Paine Museum's insurance paperwork. So it was just a matter of setting the bait.

Her hands were sweaty as she tapped Suze's contact info on her phone and hit *Call*. She refused to look nervous in front of Paul, though. She casually wiped her palms off on the side of her jeans as the phone rang.

"Laney, hi," Suze said on the other end of the line. "What's up?"

"Oh, uh." Laney swallowed, and when she spoke again, her voice was more steady. "I just wanted to tell you the good news. I, uh—that is, Mrs. Winthrop, my mom's friend—she got in touch with her main office down in Oregon, and it turns out that they've got copies of our policy on file. So they haven't all been lost after all."

If Laney hadn't already been suspicious of her, she never would have caught the very slight pause on the other end of the line, the barely perceptible hitch in Suze's voice when she said, "That's great news! Did you tell Viv yet?"

"No, I didn't. I wasn't sure if she knew what all was going on with the insurance papers, and I didn't want to bother her on her vacation," Laney said.

"Good call," Suze replied. "I've been doing daily check-ins with her. I'll let her know when I talk to her this afternoon." Then, after another moment, she said, "Laney, listen. I was thinking... maybe we shouldn't let Diane know about this."

Laney blinked. "Oh?"

"Yeah. Remember how she acted when we first told her the paintings were missing? She didn't want to call the sheriff. You pointed it out yourself."

Laney's eyebrows rose. So Suze had noticed her suspicions of

Diane the other day. That could work to Laney's advantage—if Suze thought she still suspected Diane, she'd be more likely to let her guard down.

"You're right. And she knew where our files were stored, and who our insurance agent was."

"Exactly. I think you're right, Laney," Suze said in a low voice. "Until we know for sure, I think that we shouldn't tell any of this to Diane."

"Okay, sounds good," Laney said. "I'll let you and Viv handle this."

"Thanks, Laney. It's a good thing you noticed those missing paintings. Otherwise we may never have known."

That's what you were counting on, wasn't it? Laney thought cynically. Aloud, she just thanked her and told her to keep her posted.

She hung up and turned to see that Paul had been watching her with folded arms and furrowed brows. "So?" he asked.

"She tried to deflect me to Diane. She told me not to let her know about the files in The Dalles."

"And undoubtedly, when the files go missing, it will come out that Suze 'accidentally' let it slip in front of Diane. And with you to back her up, Diane will be ruled the most likely suspect."

"Right. Which is why I need to catch Suze in the act."

Paul frowned. "I'm still not sure I love this part of your plan,

Laney. It seems to me that this is where we should turn it over to the authorities."

Laney shook her head. "They'll never believe me without evidence. You said so yourself this morning. I can't tell them about Taryn's vision. They'll think I'm crazy." When Paul opened his mouth to argue, she quickly added, "As soon as Suze or Seleste show up, I'll call the cops. They'll be there in just a minute or two. If I stay hidden, Suze will never even know I was there. It's perfectly safe."

Paul sighed wearily. "All right. But you're not going alone."

Chapter 20

The sun was low in the sky as Laney pulled into the small parking lot across the street from WPJ Insurance. It was amazing the difference in the air quality on this side of the river. Though the smell of the smoke was still strong here, the powerful gorge winds had dispersed enough of it that the air looked clear. The blanket of smoke had blown north over Washington and Canada, and west into the Willamette Valley.

You'd never know that just an hour north of here there's a fire burning that could destroy everything, Laney thought as she put her car in park.

"This seems like a good spot," she said, craning her head to look through the windshield at the office building. The businesses on this street were all located in converted Craftsman homes, freshly painted and neatly manicured like a neighborhood out of a TV show. From the vantage point of the parking lot, they had a clear view of both the front door and the narrow alley that ran between the insurance agency and the business next door; but they were far enough away that they hopefully wouldn't be immediately obvious to anyone in or around the building.

"Well, settle in," Paul said, unbuckling his seatbelt and reclining his chair slightly. "Nothing to do now but wait. And it could be quite a long wait."

As it was, it had already been quite a long drive. Although Paul's press connections had given them access to the roads that were closed to ordinary traffic—sparing them from having to make a four-hour trip through Yakima—the hour drive had been more than enough. Paul had remained uncharacteristically quiet the entire time, leaving an awkward silence hanging between them. And seeing him now, his sunglasses over his eyes and his arms folded across his chest, it seemed that he was planning to stay that way.

He'd been all too interested in talking at the restaurant this morning, Laney thought sulkily. Now it seemed he was giving her the silent treatment. She supposed she'd brought it on herself by being so evasive every time he'd tried to have a conversation with her over the last several days. But it wasn't going to make this stakeout any easier.

"I know they probably won't put in an appearance until after dark," she said.

"If they show at all," he added.

She rolled her eyes. "Right. But I figured we should get here right at closing time, just in case. You never know."

"Mmm," said Paul.

She sighed, turning up the radio and seeking around for a decent station. They sat in silence, apart from the staticky pop music drifting out of the car speakers, until well after dark.

The longer he went without speaking, the more Laney's stomach turned itself in knots. She'd managed to successfully fob him off so many times over the last three days, but now she was trapped in this small space with him. There was no escaping. He finally had her cornered, and what was he doing? Just sitting there like a log.

She leaned her forehead against the steering wheel. The tangle of thoughts that had left her such an anxious mess at breakfast were eating away at her again. Over and over she heard Carmen and Claudia's voice in her mind:

"I know you said you don't want to talk about it. But I think you need to, Laney."

"You did ask him about it, right?"

She opened and closed her mouth a half a dozen times, trying to say something. Trying to get the words out. Trying to get even *one* word out. But her tongue felt like lead.

A gust of wind shook the branches on the maple trees planted on either side of WPJ Insurance. The leaves rustled noisily, loud enough to be heard over the sound of the radio. An angled square of light from the streetlamp cast an orange glow across Paul's face as Laney watched him from the driver's seat.

"If you're going to move forward, you can't keep avoiding it."

"Paul." Her voice came out so quietly, she could barely hear it.

He didn't look at her. "Hrm?" he mumbled, still keeping his gaze riveted on the office building.

Her heart was beating so erratically she felt like it was going to leap right out of her chest. No turning back now. "Earlier," she whispered, "you said you came here for a purpose."

"Yes, I did," he replied flatly.

When he didn't go on, she added, "And the other day you said that you'd wanted the assignment in Foreston."

"Mmm."

She took a deep breath. "What did you mean?"

He gave her a sidelong glance. "What do you think I meant?"

She ground her teeth. She was trying her best here, and he was not cooperating at all. "What's with the reverse psychology?" she asked in exasperation. "Why can't you just tell me what you mean?"

He sat up, eyes wide. "Oh, so *you* want a straight answer, then? Can't handle a taste of your own medicine?"

She swallowed. Those eyes of his again. She was useless when he looked at her. "I don't know what you're talking about," she said, staring down at the steering wheel to avoid making eye contact.

He scoffed. "Right. Of course. Keep up the pretense, then."

She squeezed her eyes shut, silently counting to ten. This wasn't going at all how she'd imagined. Not that she'd imagined that it would go *well*. But it was definitely turning out even worse than she'd thought. "This is about what happened in London, isn't it?"

"Of course it is. It was never going to be anything else. You know that, right?" Paul's voice had gone from quietly churlish to raw and so full of emotion that it made Laney wince. "I thought we were serious about each other, Laney. You'd given every indication of that. And then you just *left*, with hardly a word, with hardly an explanation."

Laney's eyes burned. She blinked a couple times to try to clear them. "I did give you an explanation."

"Right, yes, of course. Over the phone, after avoiding me for a week."

She blinked again, stubbornly refusing to allow the stinging behind her eyes to develop into anything more. "I was trying to make it easier on both of us."

"You think that was easy on me?"

She turned to meet his gaze. His eyes were intense, and despite the dark of the night she could see the shine in them. The pain on his face just made this a thousand times worse.

"Look, Paul, I'm sorry, okay?" Her voice broke. "I'm sorry I just ran away, but it was five years ago! I was twenty-one years old, it's not exactly like I was the height of maturity."

"Right, and you're so much more mature now. That's why you've been avoiding having a conversation with me for the last three days. That's why I had to corner you here just to be able to *talk* to you about what happened."

"You think you're the only one this is hard for?" Laney snapped. "In case you hadn't noticed, I am not exactly good at expressing emotion in a subtle way."

"I'm aware," Paul muttered.

"I either lose my temper or I avoid. There's no in between. If you wanted subtle, you shouldn't have picked a redheaded Irish-American. If you were smart, you would have steered clear of me."

"I know."

She squeezed her eyes shut in frustration. "So why are you here, then, Paul? If you know that I'm a volatile train wreck of a human being, then what are you doing here? What is this *purpose* that you came all the way to Foreston for?"

He didn't answer immediately. He stared at her, seeming to struggle to find his words, the way Laney had when she'd started this Dumpster fire of a conversation. Then the sound of a car door slamming broke through the silence.

Laney started in alarm, whipping around in her seat to find the source of the sound. "Get down!" she hissed, shrinking back in her seat as two silhouettes came into view on the sidewalk across from the parking lot. They walked along the tree line rather than down the sidewalk, but when they passed under the streetlamp Laney could see that it was two people—women, guessing from their height—dressed all in black, with ski masks over their faces. They disappeared down the alley that ran between WPJ Insurance and the office next door.

"That's got to be them," Laney whispered.

"Right. You call the police," Paul said, quietly opening the passenger side door and slipping out.

"Wait! What are you doing?" Laney hissed.

"Keeping an eye on them so they don't slip away when the police arrive. They should hopefully have the sense to come without sirens blaring, but you can never be too certain." He pulled up the hood on his own black jacket and crept across the parking lot.

"Paul, wait!" Laney whispered frantically. Her heart pounding, she pulled out her cell phone and dialed 9-1-1. She watched in a panic as Paul crossed the street and disappeared down the same alley that Suze and Seleste, presumably, had gone down just a minute before.

"9-1-1, what's your emergency?"

Her voice shook as she told the dispatcher, "I want to report a break-in at WPJ Insurance." She kept her eyes riveted on the building in front of her, but she couldn't see any sign of Suze and Seleste or of Paul.

After she'd hung up with emergency services, she opened her door as silently as she could and listened. There was nothing but the rustling of leaves and the *whoosh* of the wind over the river. Paul had told her to wait here, but there was no sign of him now. What would happen if he got caught? Suze may be a thief, but she wasn't a murderer, right? Then again, Laney wouldn't have pegged her as a thief *or* an arsonist. There was honestly no telling what she was capable of.

Laney crept quietly from the parking lot, stopping behind the waist-high laurel hedge that separated the lot from the street. Still no sign of anyone. She was debating whether she should cross over to the office when a blur of colored light caught her eye. A fae, in the shrub. It flitted to and fro, as if trying to catch Laney's attention. She crouched in front of the shrub, trying to get a better look, when the light winked out. A moment later, she heard voices.

She held her breath, shrinking against the hedge and praying that whoever it was wouldn't notice her here. She didn't know whether the fae had been trying to warn her or if it had just been playing, but Laney knew that if she hadn't already been crouched behind the shrub, they would have seen her for sure. As they passed the bush, she heard an unfamiliar woman whisper, "If we can't find it, we'll just have to torch the place."

"I don't like it, Seleste. They already know that Mrs. Winthrop's home office was arson. This is just drawing further attention to it."

"Well, whose fault was that for being sloppy?" Seleste snapped.

"Hey, I've never had to do this before!" Suze protested. It's not my fault that Laney was being so pushy. We'd never have had to come out here in the first place if she hadn't butted in yet again."

The voices were fading now. Laney could just hear Seleste mutter, "I just want to get this taken care of and get out of this stupid state. People here are too nosy." A moment later, the car door slammed again. Laney cautiously peeked over the top of the laurel. She'd hoped that they were leaving, but it appeared they were just retrieving something from the car. She ducked back down again behind the bush. Still no sign of Paul anywhere. Where were the police? The Dalles wasn't exactly a big town; how long did it take to get here from the station?

Laney held her breath as Seleste and Suze passed again. Through the leaves of the hedge, she saw a can in Suze's hand. Turpentine. They were going to burn down the building.

Her fingernails dug into her jeans as she watched the two

women disappear down the alley. Still no sign of the police, and no sign of Paul. Was he still outside, or had he gone into the building? What would happen if they started a fire and Paul was inside?

That thought drove her across the street, trailing behind Suze and Seleste as quietly as she could. She had to stop them before they started the fire. If anything happened to Paul, Laney would never forgive herself.

Down the alley was a back door into the building. They must have picked the lock—there wasn't any obvious sign of forced entry, but the door was slightly ajar. *Idiots*, Laney thought in annoyance. What kind of insurance agency didn't have an alarm on its building? Of course, this was also the same agency that hadn't digitized any of their records, either. She supposed she shouldn't expect too much of them.

Biting down hard on the inside of her cheek, she tiptoed up the concrete steps and peeked into the door. There was no sign of the sisters inside. This appeared to be the house's former kitchen, and it looked to have been converted into a breakroom of sorts. An industrial-sized coffee pot stood on the counter, and a small, square table sat in the middle of the room, surrounded by plastic chairs with metal legs.

She slowly pushed the door open and crept inside. She could hear voices now, louder than they had been outside, talking at normal volume. Tiptoeing over to the door, she pressed her eye to the crack. Suze and Seleste were standing in the middle of the office space. Laney saw that the file cabinets that lined the office wall must have been locked, as none of the drawers were open; but they seemed to be made of wood, so there would be no hope for protection from the flames the way a metal cabinet might have provided.

"Grab everything that could possibly be flammable and pile it in front of those cabinets," Seleste was saying. Suze came over to her with an armful of couch cushions taken from the waiting area near the front door, and Seleste doused them with the paint thinner.

A noise behind Laney made her start. She looked over her shoulder to see Paul in the open door to the alley. He stared at Laney in alarm. "What are you doing?" he mouthed.

Thank goodness! Laney thought in relief. He wasn't in the house—so even if they managed to set the office on fire, he wouldn't be trapped. Now, where were the police? Quietly, she tiptoed back toward the door.

Under her foot, a floorboard squeaked noisily. Panicked, she froze.

"What was that?" Suze asked.

Laney's eyes widened. Busted.

"Run," Paul whispered. It took Laney's feet an agonizing moment to obey. She sprinted across the kitchen, making it out the door just as the door from the kitchen to the office swung open.

"Stop them!" Seleste shouted as Laney burst into the alley.

"Run!" Paul urged again, grabbing Laney's hand and pulling her toward the street. His strides were much longer than hers, though, knocking her off balance. She made it three steps before tripping over her feet on the uneven pavement and staggering into Paul. He caught her, managing to keep them from falling face-first onto the asphalt; but her stumble gave Seleste enough time to reach the door to the alley.

"Freeze!" she snapped. Laney looked up to see Seleste aiming a handgun at them. She swallowed hard.

Slowly, Paul raised his hands, and Laney followed suit. Suze joined her sister in the doorway and groaned. "Laney. I should have known." She shook her head. "Couldn't you just leave well enough alone? We didn't want to hurt anybody."

"You don't think stealing from the museum is hurting someone?" Laney scoffed.

Suze rolled her eyes. "Nobody cares about a podunk little museum out in the middle of nowhere. No one would ever have even noticed those paintings had been swapped in the first place if you hadn't butted in—and kept right on butting in and butting in. Now look what you've done."

"Get over here," Seleste said. "Nice and easy. Keep your hands where I can see them."

Laney and Paul trudged back into the kitchen and Suze shut the door behind them. "I'd been planning on setting Diane up to take the fall. But I guess it's going to have to be you," she said.

"Me?" Laney squeaked.

"What else are the authorities going to think when they find your remains here? You set the fire at Mrs. Winthrop's, and you came here to finish the job, but you just didn't get out quickly enough."

"You can't be serious, Suze," Laney protested. "You're not like this. You're not a killer."

"I wasn't an arsonist, either," Suze snapped. "You just bring it out in me, I guess."

"And the police are supposed to buy that I was in on it?" Paul said dubiously.

Suze shrugged. "No one noticed that the paintings were gone until you showed up. But if you find that theory unconvincing, we could always dump your body in the Columbia. I'm easy."

"Into the office," said Seleste. "Let's go."

Hands still raised, they started to follow Suze into the office, Seleste coming up in the rear. They only made it a few steps, though, when Laney, temper flaring, impulsively reached up and yanked on Suze's long, dark ponytail as hard as she could. Suze screamed in surprise. Paul didn't waste a second. He whipped around, grabbing one of the plastic chairs next to the table and swinging it at Seleste. The chair connected hard with her wrist and she cried out in pain, dropping the gun. Paul and Seleste both dove for it, scuffling on the floor.

"Laney, run!" Paul shouted. She hesitated for a moment, not wanting to leave him here with them when a gun was involved. But he yelled, "Run!" a second time, and this time she bolted. Suze was hot on her heels, though. She tore out of the alley and around the corner, but then there was a sharp tug on the back of her head, and she fell, landing painfully on her left arm.

"See how you like it!" Suze spat. Laney kicked out with her right foot, connecting with Suze's ankle and knocking her off balance. Suze tumbled, landing hard on Laney's legs. They scratched and kicked at each other, Laney desperate to get away before Seleste reappeared with the gun.

"Help!" Laney shouted at the top of her lungs. She clawed at the grass frantically. *Somebody, something, please—please—help me!*

Under her fingers, there was a light rumbling, and the air filled with an odd hissing noise. Then a stream of water burst up from the ground beside her, spraying Suze directly in the face. Laney scrambled away from her, staggering to her feet. Water was spraying all around. The underground sprinkler system had suddenly turned on, pelting them.

Suze screamed in frustration as Paul burst around the corner.

He held Seleste's upper arm firmly with his left hand, and in his right was the handgun. Laney let out a sigh of relief. Paul was safe. He'd gotten the gun. It was over.

Just then, a bright light filled the air all around them. Laney winced, squeezing her eyes closed, but that did little to offset the spotlight's effect.

"Freeze! Police!" a voice boomed over a loudspeaker.

Oh, now *they show up!* Laney thought in annoyance. But it didn't matter. At her feet, Suze slowly raised her hands. Beside Paul, Seleste did the same.

It was over. Laney let out a breath, raising her own hands as the officers approached them. It was over. They'd done it. The art thieves had been caught.

Chapter 21

It was after midnight when Laney and Paul finally staggered up the stairs to her apartment. After a trip to the police station, where they'd explained everything, they'd been told they were free to go—after getting a stern lecture about interfering with a criminal investigation, and how dangerous that could be. As if they hadn't already learned that lesson the hard way. Paul had assured her that lectures like those were par for the course; he had routinely made interfering with criminal investigations his business back during his uVer days.

The wind had been high as they drove across the bridge back to the Washington side. In her headlights, the branches of the trees around them swayed intensely... until they gave way to the burned sections. There, naked trunks stood black and smoldering.

Seeing the devastation made the fire seem more real to Laney than it had until now, even with the blanket of smoke a constant reminder. The wind was whipping like it did when a storm was blowing in, but it had no coolness to it, and the air felt dry rather than moist.

She'd gotten so wrapped up with the art theft and trying to catch Suze and Seleste in the act that the threat of the fire had been pushed to the back of her mind. But they weren't out of the woods yet. Until the fire was completely contained, there was always a chance it could still spread. It wasn't yet time to celebrate.

"Remember, Monty said he'd call me if anything changed," Paul had said as Laney stared glumly at the burned husks as they drove down the empty highway. Paul had pre-filmed some canned fire updates for the network that afternoon before they left Foreston. As long as the situation didn't change, they'd have plenty of footage for the network to run during its periodic updates. The fact that Paul hadn't heard anything meant that Foreston was still safe, as hard as that had been for Laney to accept, seeing the destruction around her.

When they got back, Laney unlocked the door and flipped on the light switch. Though they'd only been there two nights, it already felt weird that Carmen and Claudia (and Sofia, of course) were gone. She'd gotten a text from Carmen while she and Paul were at the police station, letting her know that Josh's flight had arrived safely. Laney wondered how long it would be before they returned to Foreston.

"Reckon I can sleep on the sofa tonight, then," Paul pointed out as he came into the apartment.

"Oh, yeah. That's right," Laney said, feeling oddly hollow inside.

Paul sank onto the couch while Laney took her shoes off, relishing the freedom of bare feet. She felt like she'd been hit up and down by a baseball bat. Considering the struggle she'd gone through with Suze on WPJ's front lawn, that probably wasn't too far off the mark.

"We didn't do too bad out there," she commented, running a hand through her hair. It had mostly dried by now, after being blasted with the sprinklers, but she still felt limp and wrung out. She needed to shower, but she was honestly too tired.

"Yeah, that was a bit of good luck that their sprinklers went off right when they did," said Paul.

"Right. Luck," Laney said. She felt odd about it, somehow. That the sprinklers had gone off just then—right after she'd called out for help. When she put her hand on the grass... it had felt almost like she'd called it, somehow. But that was impossible. Her faery blessing only worked when she was sewing, right?

Paul was watching her quietly from the couch. He sighed, leaning forward with his elbows on his knees. "You know, I was afraid I was going to lose you tonight. When Seleste pulled out that gun. I told you to wait in the car. Why didn't you listen to me?"

Laney bit her lip. "I got worried about you. I didn't know where you'd gone, but when Suze and Seleste went by with that can of turpentine... I was scared you might have been in the office, that you'd get trapped when they set the fire."

"So you came looking for me?" he asked.

Laney kept her feet trained on the floor, nodding silently.

Paul didn't respond for a minute. When Laney finally ventured a glance up at him, he was smiling. He patted the empty space beside him on the couch. Hesitantly, she came over.

"Laney, listen," he said quietly as she sat down. "Last night... I heard what you said to Carmen and Claudia." She flushed crimson, but he quickly went on, "You have to know, I didn't kiss that woman. I didn't even *know* her! She'd tagged along with my mates to the pub and she was drunk out of her mind. I kept trying to give her a wide berth, but she wouldn't leave me alone. She kept throwing herself at me. I suppose she was just desperate to be some kind of uVer groupie." His voice was urgent, pleading. He put his hand on her knee. "I don't know what you saw, but Laney, I promise you, I never kissed that woman."

Laney swallowed, looking down at his hand. "I know," she whispered.

Paul stared at her. "What?"

She nodded. "Even by the time I'd made it back to my room, I knew you hadn't. I knew you wouldn't do that, Paul. You weren't like that." She swallowed. "But I also knew that it wasn't going to stop. You were just getting more and more popular on uView, and more girls were coming up to you, and there was that fan Wiki with all that personal information on it, and…" She trailed off, looking down. "There was a page about me on it. On the Wiki."

He sighed, leaning back against the couch. "I know. When I found out about it, I made the site administrator take it down."

She nodded. "I figured. I saw it was gone by the time I got home. But I just… I couldn't handle it. It was all too much. And if there were going to be girls like that throwing themselves at you, how long would it take before you realized that I just couldn't compete?" Her eyes stung, and this time no amount of blinking would hold back the tears. "I'm nothing special. You had this great career in front of you, and I was just majoring in English lit because I couldn't think of anything better to do. And now look at me. Back in this, this… dictionary example of 'sleepy little town.' Working in my parents' alterations shop." A hot tear slid down her cheek. "Why would someone like you waste your time on someone like me when you could have anyone?"

Paul looked at her earnestly, shaking his head. "Laney, I'm not a movie star or a celebrity. I'm a just one out of a dozen field reporters at the network, and before that I was just a midlist uVer with a handful of internet nerds as my fanbase. I'm not anything special. I don't know why you're treating me like I am."

"You are special, Paul. You've always been special to me." Another tear escaped down her face. *Too special for me to hold on to.*

Paul sighed. "All right. You want to know the reason I came here? My purpose for asking for the Foreston assignment?" He reached out, placing a hand on her cheek, turning it to face him. He took her hand with his free one. "This. Right here. This conversation. Because it's been five years. I tried my hardest to move on, but I couldn't. You think you wouldn't compare to any other girls? The truth is, I've *tried* dating other girls since you. And none of them could compare to *you*." He ran a thumb over her cheek, wiping away another tear. "Yes, you're short-tempered and impulsive and you don't cope well with your emotions. But you're also loyal and determined and feisty, and you're the only one I want to wake up next to every day. I love you, Laney. I never stopped loving you."

Laney sniffled, another tear escaping down her cheek. She couldn't breathe, couldn't think. Paul loved her. Impossibly, after everything she'd done, he still loved her.

Somehow, she managed to whisper, "I never stopped loving you, either."

He leaned in close, pressing his lips gently against hers. She closed her eyes, snaking her arm around his neck. Five years. She'd dreamed of this for five years, even though she'd denied it every day. There could never be anyone else for her. No one she would ever love as much as Paul.

He pulled away, just slightly, grinning against her mouth. His fingers caught in her tangled, messy hair. "And from now on, we're not going to avoid our problems, right? We're going to talk about them."

Laney laughed, brushing her lips against his jaw. "I'll try."

"I'll hold you to that," Paul said. "I'm not going to let you run halfway across the world again."

"Never. You'll always know where to find me."

Paul kissed her again, and again, and again.

Chapter 22

She was walking through the woods.

Though she knew all the trails around the Paine property like the back of her hand, this one looked different somehow. Unfamiliar. It wound through an unkempt rose garden, across overgrown, uneven cobblestones. Past a fallen log where sunlight streamed through the canopy overhead, leaving dappled patches on the ground. The homey smell of dry grass reached her nose on a gentle breeze, and all around her, the sounds of nature hummed.

She sat on the fallen log, looking around at the familiar-yet-strange woods. In the branches over her head, blurry figures danced to and fro, leaving streaks of color and light in their wake. Their voices were like chattering squirrels and chirping birds. Fae were all around her in this place. Hundreds, maybe even thousands of them.

She let out a dreamy sigh. "I wish I could see you," she said.

There was a rustling at her feet. She looked down, her eyes widening as she saw it, peeking out between blades of tall, overgrown grass. Clear as day. Her skin prickled with gooseflesh. A tiny, humanoid figure, with skin as green as a bright spring leaf. It had a sly, angular face, and a mound of leaves on the top of its head that could have been a hat or could have been hair—did fae have hair? Laney had never seen one clearly enough to tell. But she knew, instinctively, that this creature was indeed a fae.

She could see a fae. Clear as day.

The creature shoved the tall grass aside and came to stand at her feet. It crossed its arms, looking up at her with an arched brow, an oddly human gesture. "You could see us, if you put your mind to it," said the fae.

Laney's jaw dropped. "You can talk? But Taryn said—"

The creature ignored her. "Has anyone ever told you that you're stubborn?"

She crossed her own arms, peering down at it. "Many times."

It shook its head. "Humans. Tell me, when did you decide that you couldn't See as well as your sister?"

"I never *decided* it," Laney protested. "It's just true."

The creature came over, hopping up onto the fallen log with an effortless leap and sitting down beside Laney. "You know, the Sight works two ways."

Laney furrowed her eyebrows. "What do you mean?"

"I mean it's give and take. We give the gift, and you accept the gift. But it won't work if you don't want to accept it."

"I do want to accept it!" Laney cried.

The creature leaned back on its elbows, crossing its knobbly knees. "Do you believe?" it asked.

Laney stared at it in confusion. "What?"

"Do you believe that you could see as well as your sister?"

It watched Laney as she hesitated.

"There, you see," it said, as if she'd proved its point.

"It's not that," Laney argued. "Taryn is special."

"Taryn is special, and you're not?" said the fae.

Laney opened her mouth, then paused. She'd said it to Paul, hadn't she? She wasn't anything special. She couldn't compare.

But Paul said she was special. Just like Paul was special to her.

The fae smirked at her and said, "Maybe you should work on believing it."

The clearing around her grew dim, as if the sun had passed behind a cloud. And then, lights began to shine, one by one. Different colors, like twinkling Christmas lights. Like the battery-operated strands Taryn had in her dorm room. She didn't call them Christmas lights, though. What did she say they were?

That's right. Fairy lights.

All around her, the lights grew brighter, forming shapes,

silhouettes. And then her eyes focused, and she saw them all around. Long, narrow faeries with gossamer wings; squat, round-featured gnomes with bulbous noses. Tiny pixies, barely bigger than bumblebees. Fae of every shape and size imaginable, all the colors of the forest, looking at her. And she could see them, as clear as day. Their voices became more clear, speaking that strange language that she'd only ever heard snatches of throughout her life. At first she couldn't understand it, but the longer she listened, the more words began to become clear to her.

Laney.

Help us.

You have to help us.

We helped you. Now you have to help us.

She looked around in confusion. "Help you?" she called to the trees? "Help you with what?" She turned back to the fae on the stump beside her, asking, "What are they talking about?"

But the green fae was gone.

Alarmed, she got to her feet, looking up into the trees. "What do you need help with?" she called.

The sky grew dark, and a shadow fell over her. Startled, she turned, and suddenly the clearing had changed. It was no longer the strange, unfamiliar place she'd been just a moment before. Now she was in the hollow tree clearing. The fallen log had become a park bench, and the tall grass behind it had changed into the neatly manicured flowerbeds lining the trail at the museum. As she stared, the dogwood tree began to glow, orange embers drifting into the air above it. Smoke choked her lungs.

There was a shrill, beeping sound, like that of a fire alarm.

Help us. Please.

With a gasp, Laney jerked awake.

Disoriented, she tried to get her bearings. Her neck was stiff. She lifted her head slightly and found that she'd fallen asleep on the couch beside Paul, her face in his chest. The shrill, beeping sound came again, and she realized that it was the sound her cell phone had made on Friday when the first set of emergency alerts had come in.

Oh, no. Please, no.

She sat up quickly, disentangling herself from Paul, who startled awake. "Wh-what?" he mumbled groggily. "What's going on?"

"The fire," she said, hands shaking as she reached for her cell phone on the coffee table. She pressed the lock button, looking at the message on the screen as it lit up.

Emergency alert—prepare for action. The city of FORESTON, WASHINGTON *is under immediate evacuation notice.*

She turned to Paul, who had pulled his own phone out of his jeans pocket. His eyes were still slightly out-of-focus as he looked at the screen, but they sharpened almost instantly. "It's three-thirty. Monty called me twenty minutes ago and I missed it. The fire jumped the control line. It's headed for town."

"We have to go," Laney said, abandoning her phone on the coffee table and racing to grab her shoes. She hopped on one foot to shove one, then the other on.

Paul nodded, getting to his feet. "Do you have a bag packed?"

She shook her head. "We have to get to the hollow tree."

Paul stared at her incredulously. "Excuse me?"

"Paul, trust me. The warren is in danger."

"What, did someone call you?"

"Yes, someone called me," she said seriously. "The fae. They told me they're in danger. They need my help."

"I'm sorry, weren't we just in a police station five hours ago learning the lesson about leaving matters like this up to the authorities? Remember the part where we very nearly were killed?"

"I know, I know." She grabbed his hand, looking up at him imploringly. "But, Paul, in cases like this, I *am* the authorities. This is my job. I was given a gift by the fae, and it comes with responsibility."

He stared at her for a long moment, his expression unreadable, and for a horrible instant Laney thought that maybe he hadn't been telling the truth all those times he told her he believed in her Sight, in the fae and in her family's faery blessings.

But then he nodded, grabbing his jacket off the couch and pulling it on.

"Let's go," he said.

The streets of Foreston were pandemonium as people hurried to leave town, a line of cars streaming down Main Street toward the northbound highway. Laney's car was the only one heading in the opposite direction. With no regard to speed limits, she careened through town toward Paine Parkway as fast as she dared.

The sky over the woods glowed a sickening orange. The fire was close. Way, way too close.

She didn't head to the parking lot. Instead, she stopped her car as close to the garden entrance as she could, leaping out of the car and running down the trail into the trees. The air around them was filled with the same horrible screeches and howls they'd heard at Mrs. Winthrop's house yesterday.

"Those are the fae?" Paul asked, choking on the smoke as they ran. Neither of them had thought to grab their masks. There wasn't time.

A gust of wind rattled the branches over her head. "That's them!" Laney called back to him.

The path was illuminated orange. It glowed between the trunks of the trees. *We're not going to make it*, Laney thought in despair. It was too close, too close, too close.

They burst into the clearing with the hollow tree. In the orange glow, Laney could see a figure crouched in front of the warren. In a panic, her mind screamed, *Not Taryn, not Taryn, not Taryn.* If the fae had called her sister here, too, it would destroy her family. She couldn't guarantee that she was going to make it out of this. Losing one daughter would be bad enough, but two—

The figure turned to look at Laney, and her eyes widened in surprise. "Bob!" she exclaimed.

The old man smirked at the sight of her. "So, you do care," he said in a low, gravelly voice.

"Bob, what are you doing here?" Laney demanded.

He gestured to the hollow tree. "Someone has to look after this place and the creatures living in it," he said.

Suddenly, the pieces fell into place. "Bob," Laney breathed, then choked on the smoke. Between coughs, she asked, "Can you see the fae?"

Bob said nothing. He just nodded curtly, once.

He could see the fae. And he knew Laney and Taryn could, too. He must have. All the cryptic hints, the riddles. The odd way he behaved, talking to things that weren't there—no. Not things that weren't there. *Fae.* Laney hadn't been able to see them. Taryn probably would have, but she'd never dared get close enough to Bob to actually look. They'd just assumed. Assumed he was crazy, that he was weird, that they should keep their distance.

But all along, Bob had been looking after the woods in a way that Laney had failed to, time and time again.

"Right. We need to protect the tree, then," Paul said behind Laney's shoulder. When she glanced at him, he added, "Right? This is the warren?"

Laney nodded, smiling in spite of herself. "Right."

"We need to get it wet. This whole area," said Bob. "Wet wood won't burn."

"Are there any hoses about?" asked Paul.

"Here, in the flowerbeds," Laney said. Concealed in a large urn behind one of the park benches was the spigot that usually connected to soaker hoses threaded around the landscaping. But there was also a regular hose coiled up in the urn as well. "There's another one on that side," she said to Paul, gesturing to the bench across the clearing. She started unscrewing the soaker from the nozzle with her hand. It had been tightly attached, and her palms stung as she wrenched the metal fastener as quickly as she could. There was no time for caution. The air around her was hot, like when you open an oven door and the heat rushes into the room. The skin on her face stung, and she coughed as she breathed in smoke and ash.

"Got it," she said when she finally had attached the regular garden hose to the faucet. She cranked the handle as far open as it would go. Water gushed forth from the hose's end.

"Get everything wet," she called to Paul as he turned on his own hose. "As wet as you possibly can. Start with the hollow tree and fan out as far as the hose will stretch."

She pressed her thumb into the hose's spout, creating a spray of water. It rained down on Bob like a thunderstorm. He stayed crouched at the base of the tree, murmuring reassuringly to the blurred glowing figures that congregated around him, climbing up onto his shoulders and nesting in his hair.

"That's enough, fan out," Paul said.

"Are you sure?" Laney asked, looking at the tree hesitantly. What if they hadn't gotten it saturated enough? What if it was still dry enough to burn?

"Trust me. We need to get the rest of the area. The best way to protect the tree is to keep the fire from getting close to it in the first place."

She nodded, fanning out with her hose, soaking everything that could ever possibly burn with as much water as she could. Like the rains that had so long abandoned this place, drying it out like a tinderbox. The ground drank the water greedily, and she continued to give it more, until little puddles formed around the bases of the dainty currant shrubs and the thick, lush hydrangeas, the alyssum and water hyssop that covered the ground in the flowerbeds and the ferns that sprouted in the wildness beyond. She aimed the spray up into the trees as high as it would go, soaking the leaves and the pine needles, causing the blurred figures of the watching fae to shriek in surprise as they were pelted with a stream of water.

The wind tossed the spray back at her, soaking her just like the sprinkler had this evening. Had it just been this evening? It felt like it had been ages ago. She couldn't believe she'd been so wrapped up in finding those paintings, had thought it was such a priority. What had been the point? Would the museum still even be standing tomorrow? Even if it was, if Suze's house went up in flames, the paintings would be lost forever anyway. All that effort for nothing.

The air was hot. It burned. It burned and stung and choked the breath right out of her.

"That's enough! It's too close, Laney. Leave it! Bring the hose back to the tree," Paul called.

Laney nodded, hurrying back over to where he and Bob stood. The hose still gushed water, creating a tiny river when she set it down at the base of the tree. The warren was glowing, like it had in her dream. The sight of it turned her stomach.

"There's nothing more we can do," Paul said. "We can't stay here, Laney. It's too dangerous."

"I won't leave!" Laney argued. "They called me. They asked me to help them. I can't leave them."

Bob nodded approvingly. "She's accepted her role as caretaker," he growled.

Paul stared between them, sighing resignedly. "I won't leave you, Laney," he said.

She took his hand. "We have to trust the magic," she said. "We have to trust it, and hope for the best."

The flames were close now. She could see them between the trunks of the trees that edged the clearing, licking at the grass and ferns, climbing up the trees to the dry leaves Laney had been unable to reach with the hose.

She squeezed her eyes shut, sinking to her knees next to Bob. This couldn't be the end. It just couldn't.

Her fingers touched the ground, the short tufts of wild grass growing between the roots of the dogwood. The feel of it reminded her—at the insurance agency tonight. She'd asked for help... and help had come. Just like the little faery in the laurel hedge that had warned her before Suze and Seleste emerged from the alley. Just like when Taryn had been trying to read the painting for a memory. And just like the brownie who'd alerted her to the missing paintings in the first place.

Her powers only worked when she was sewing, right? That's what she'd always believed.

She suddenly remembered the strange green fae from her dream. What had it said?

"When did you decide that you couldn't See as well as your sister?"

Probably around the same time that she'd *decided* that her powers only worked when sewing. Bob had told her before that her stubbornness blinded her. And the fae had said that the gift had to be accepted, not just given.

"*Do you believe?*"

Laney squared her shoulders, pressing her hand firmly to the ground between the gnarled roots of the dogwood. "I believe," she said out loud.

Paul looked at her in surprise. "What's that, love?"

Beside her, Bob grinned. "That's it," he said, clamping his hand down on Laney's shoulder. "That's it."

Laney nodded, closing her eyes and feeling the energy passing from her chest, radiating out through her shoulder and down her arm, through her fingers, into the ground. The roots of the tree spread out far beyond the tree's footprint. They went deep underground, out across the clearing, tangling and entwining with the trees around it—ancient white oaks, towering pines. Yews and maples and firs. All the trees of the forest. She felt them beneath her, and she felt them in her.

"Help us," she said. "Save these woods. Save Foreston."

The dogwood glowed. Not the orange of her dream, the orange of flames about to consume its ancient, dry bark. It glowed pastel colors, like fairy lights. It glowed greens and browns, golds and coppers. All the colors of the forest, of the trees and the flowers that bloomed all throughout the year.

Laney blinked, and the world around her seemed to come into

focus. They were there. The fae. All the species of the fae that she could ever imagine. Everything that Taryn had ever told her about, everything she'd read about in books and seen in illustrations. They were all here, crouched beside her, around her. All over the dogwood tree, clinging to its bark like dainty butterflies and sturdy centipedes. They were in the branches of the trees above her, nestled in the leaves of the hydrangeas, peeking out between vines of ivy and tendrils of water hyssop. As she watched, they stretched out their little hands—their fingers long and slender, short and stubby, gnarled and knobby, and everything in between. Their forms began to glow. She felt their energy pouring into her, stronger and more powerful than anything she'd ever experienced. She was a conduit, and her intention had the power to change reality.

This was her blessing. And this moment was the reason she'd been given it.

She closed her eyes and released the energy into the ground.

"Save the woods," she whispered.

Smoke still hung in the still air as the sun rose. But the flames were gone. All that remained was the smoldering ashes of what had already burned.

Laney sat weakly on the ground at the foot of the hollow tree, her back braced against its trunk. Paul sat beside her, his arm around her shoulders, steadying her. Fae climbed all over her, tickling like ants, but she didn't mind. She smiled as one climbed on her shoulder and began braiding a tiny section of her hair.

She could See. She could See everything now.

I guess I always could have. I just didn't believe in myself enough to try.

Paul's phone chimed in his pocket. He pulled it out with his free hand, reading the message had just come in. "They've got the fire contained outside of Foreston," he said, looking up at Laney. "The branch of the fire that had spread up this way appears to have burned itself out. They're not really sure why," he added with a snort. "But I'm sure there's some sort of scientific explanation. Regardless, there seems to have been minimal damage to the town itself."

Laney sighed with relief. She felt more exhausted than she'd ever felt in her life. A tiny blue faery the same color as the hydrangea blossoms alighted on her leg and patted her knee comfortingly. She smiled at it.

"I hope my parents are okay," she said. "I left my cell phone back at the apartment. Taryn's probably going to kill me."

"She'll understand," Paul said, leaning over to kiss her lightly on her lips.

Bob trundled back into the clearing then, a metal bowl in his hands with steam wafting out of it. He'd left about twenty minutes before, citing the need to check on his tent. "Got you some nourishment," he grunted, shoving the bowl into her hands. Canned beef stew.

"Thanks," Laney said. Beef stew wasn't her typical breakfast of choice, but she had a feeling that after this night, it was going to be the most delicious thing she'd ever tasted.

Paul's phone chimed again. He looked at it and sighed. "Duty calls," he said, getting to his feet and brushing the dirt off his knees. "We managed to put off updating our coverage, but the network will have my head if I don't give a proper report now."

"It's fine," Laney said, looking up at him. "Do you need a ride?"

"No, Monty and Ashley are on their way here. I'll just film the update at the entrance to the garden, if that's all right."

Laney nodded weakly. He leaned down to kiss her again, and she hooked her fingers in his T-shirt, holding him there for just a moment longer. When they parted, she said, "I need to get back and check on everyone. Make sure Mom and Dad and Taryn are okay. I just need another minute."

Paul smiled at her. "Take all the time you need."

She took a few more bites of beef stew, the food making her feel a bit less shaky and weak. "Thanks for this, Bob," she said.

The old man was stooped in front of the flowerbeds with his back to her, murmuring to a gnome at his feet. He glanced over his shoulder and muttered a "Welcome" at her.

When she'd finished the bowl, setting it down on the ground beside her, she stretched her legs out and watched Bob as he looked up at a pixy on the branch above him. He gently reached out his hand, and the pixy flitted over, landing on his index finger and allowing him to gently stroke its head.

"Do you have a faery blessing, Bob?" Laney asked.

Bob nodded soundlessly.

"Well, what is it?"

He looked over his shoulder at her again, shaking his head. "None of your business," he grunted.

Laney smirked, leaning back against the tree and looking up at the sky. Between the branches overhead, it was a clear, cloudless blue.

Finally, she stood, holding onto the hollow tree for support, and looked up into the lopsided branches. She was about to turn when a splash of white between the green leaves on the living side caught her eye. Furrowing her brows, she walked around the trunk, peering into the branches above her.

Fae bustled along the branches, flitting between the leaves, but that wasn't what had caught Laney's attention. It was the delicate buds of white flowers, partially opened, spreading their petals to the sun.

The dogwood tree was blooming.

Laney smiled to herself, walking back down the path toward the house.

Epilogue

Two years later...

"Mrs. Nelson, which booth number did you have us at again?"

Laney looked up from the box she was rummaging through to see one of the designers' assistants standing in front of her, her arms laden with garment bags stamped *Dina's Boutique*.

"Booth Six," she replied, pointing to a table near the tent's entrance.

"Great, thanks," the girl said, gesturing for a lanky boy behind her—whose arms were filled with even *more* garment bags—to follow her to the booth.

Laney sighed, looking around the large, airy pole tent. Finally, after two years of planning, setup was underway for the return of the fashion show.

It had taken a long time before Foreston had started to look like itself again. The fire in the national forest hadn't managed to reach one hundred percent containment until the fall rains had come, putting out the remaining low-heat fires that had been smoldering in the undergrowth. And even though the town itself had remained relatively untouched by the fire, reminders of the Blackberry Creek Fire, as it had come to be known, were still present everywhere. From the scorched hills along the highway to the state forestry department still working to remove dangerously unstable burned-out tree trunks, the devastation the fire had wrought was impossible to forget.

Still, it could have been much worse. New growth, lush and green, was already beginning to fill the gaps in the charred earth. Even though much of the forest had been lost, a new forest was forming in its wake. Most importantly, the town, the museum, and most of Paine Woods had been spared. Though many houses in Fernhill had been damaged or destroyed, miraculously, Carmen and Josh's home had remained unscathed. And Laney's parents' home had also managed to avoid the path of the fire, something Laney was eternally grateful for.

She still remembered how angry her family had been with her the night of 'the incident,' as it had come to be known. When the emergency alert text had come in, Taryn, Matthew, and their parents had all tried to get through to Laney, but with her cell phone left back at her apartment, she'd had no way of reaching them. It was probably for the best—she wouldn't have been able to answer with everything else going on, and if they'd been able to track her location and had seen that she was at the museum... it wouldn't have been pretty.

She was just grateful that Aden and Nancy had never found out exactly what had gone down in The Dalles that evening. She was in enough trouble for risking her life for the hollow tree, even though her whole family acknowledged the importance of protecting the warren. If they knew that she'd *also* risked her life by butting into a criminal investigation... Laney didn't know if it was possible to ground a twenty-eight-year-old (well, twenty-six at the time), especially if she didn't live in the same house as them, but she suspected that her parents would have found a way.

She looked around at the tent, watching as the designers set up their booths, sorting out the clothes the models would wear in the fashion show from the ones that would be on display for shoppers to peruse. The tent was arranged like the layers of an onion—the booths around the outside of the tent, then the rows of chairs for the spectators, and in the center, the catwalk. It was nothing fancy; not a raised platform or stage, just a simple aisle lined with velvet cordons. But the sight of it all coming together still made Laney beam with pride. Things hadn't gone to plan by a long shot. If things had worked out like they were supposed to, they'd be celebrating the fifth annual fashion show this year.

But if things had worked out like they were supposed to, everything would be different now. And Laney wouldn't trade the life she had now for anything.

Outside the tent, Laney heard a car door slam, and then the sound of barking growing ever louder. She came out of the tent to see a floppy-eared red Doberman bounding toward her, pulling hard on the leash of his owner—her brother, Matthew. A short distance behind him, Laney's parents had a more sedate Bailey on his lead.

"What are you guys doing here?" Laney asked, laughing as Tucker, the Doberman, eagerly sniffed at her skirt, at her knees, at her sandals, and everything to do with her. She stroked his soft ears and he looked up at her, wagging his stub tail.

"We wanted to see if you needed any help," Nancy said.

"We probably would have been of more help without these two knuckleheads," Aden added wryly. Bailey had stopped in a sunny patch of the grass and was pawing at it.

"Hey, Bailey's being good," Matthew pointed out. "It's just Idiot Stick here who's the problem."

"You're harsh on Tucker," Laney said, attempting to disentangle herself from the Doberman's leash, which had gotten wrapped around her ankles as he'd circled her. "You're going to give him a complex."

The truth was, Laney was glad to see her brother. Visits from Matthew were going to be all the more rare now that he'd moved two hours south of Eugene, to a tiny little town called Riddle. None of them could figure out why he'd decided to go there, of all places—in the middle of nowhere and even farther from his family and friends than he'd been before. But he'd said he'd had one of his *feelings* that Riddle was where he was meant to go, and everyone knew better than to argue with him on that point.

"If you keep going south, you're going to end up in California," Taryn had teased the last time Matthew had visited, back in June. But Matthew had just shuddered and said, "Never."

"Is your sister here?" Aden asked, glancing down at Bailey, who, after circling it twenty-three times, had at last settled down in the sunny patch of grass.

Laney nodded. "She's in the bridal room with Carmen and Claudia. They're modeling for the show, so they're trying out different ensembles to make sure they fit."

Taryn had graduated from Washington State a little over a year ago and had begun working at the Penngrove full-time. Laney suspected that the owners were planning on offering her a manager position soon, but Taryn was still holding out the hope of opening her own bed-and-breakfast.

"Do you think you'll stay in Foreston forever, like Laney?" Matthew had asked her, during the same conversation about his own move to Riddle.

"I dunno. I'm undecided," Taryn had admitted. "Maybe you'll get one of your trademark Feelings and let me know where it is I'm supposed to go."

They'd laughed about it, but Laney half wondered if Taryn was being serious. She'd given it some thought over the past couple years, as she'd learned more about herself, her powers, and about the fae. Matthew didn't have Sight—he insisted that he still didn't. But she remembered what the fae from her dream had said, that gifts worked both ways. Had Matthew also been given a gift, one that he didn't yet understand?

The dream she'd had that night had stayed with her, not dulling as time went on. She'd never seen a fae like that one anywhere in the Paine Woods. Had it been a figment of her imagination? Or was it a real fae that she just hadn't encountered yet? She couldn't shake the feeling that she hadn't seen the last of that creature...

"You didn't tell me there were going to be dogs at this event!" A shrill voice jolted Laney out of her reverie, and she turned her head to see Diane standing, aghast, at the head of the steps leading from the tennis court to the house.

Laney sighed. Diane. She may not have been a criminal, but she was still a cantankerous old bat—and just as involved with the goings-on at the Paine Museum as ever.

"I wasn't planning on it. They just showed up," Laney protested.

"Now, Diane, leave them be! They aren't bothering anyone!" Viv appeared over Diane's shoulder, pushing past her and bustling down the stairs to greet the dogs. "Look what little sweeties they are." She stroked Tucker's ears, then crouched to pet Bailey, who wriggled over to her on his belly, not bothering to stand up from his sunny spot.

"Well, they better not trample the flowerbeds," Diane huffed. "I've got a wedding in the Tea Garden next weekend, and I don't want to have to explain to my bride that her big day's been ruined because some people don't know how to curb their dogs."

Viv looked up at Laney and rolled her eyes. Turning to Diane, she said, "The Tea Garden's never looked this good, and you know it."

Diane huffed again, turning and marching back up to the house. Laney snickered to herself. The *reason* the gardens were looking so much better than usual was a point of contention between Diane and the rest of the staff. After the fire, when the town came together to rebuild, there had been a lot of cleanup work needed on the museum grounds. And Laney knew just the person for the job, someone who put the welfare of the woods and the whole of nature before himself.

Which is how Bob became the official groundskeeper of the

Paine Estate. They'd converted the original caretaker's cottage from back when the Paine family had lived here—which was being used as storage for the museum—into a comfortable tiny home for him. Now Bob could spend the rest of his days living here and looking after the warren and the rest of the woods, without having to stay in a tent.

Diane, of course, had not been a fan of making Crazy Old Bob a permanent fixture at the Paine Museum. But that, in Laney's opinion, just made it an even better idea. And Viv was right: the gardens had never looked better.

"How's setup going, Laney?" Viv asked, still kneeling in the grass rubbing Bailey's tummy. Tucker watched enviously.

"Everything seems to be going smoothly," Laney said, holding up her crossed fingers.

"It's going to be a hit," Aden said reassuringly.

"You certainly have worked hard enough," Nancy pointed out.

"Exactly. And sales for this year's event blew our projected tickets for two years ago out of the water," Viv said. "Guess that news feature really did give us a boost after all."

Laney grinned. Of course, the story that had eventually aired on *Around America* was drastically different than the one that had originally been planned. Rather than focusing on the museum and the fashion show, the story instead became about how a tiny community in rural Washington had come together to recover from a crisis. Most of the original footage had been scrapped, apart from Monty's drone footage and the shots of Main Street.

But it was just as well. After everything that had happened, Laney realized that she didn't think she really wanted to share the magic of Foreston with the outside world. She was happy keeping Foreston just the way it was.

Of course, the feature's focus wasn't the only thing that had changed. In the end, it had been hosted by Gloria Shellburg after all. It turned out that Paul Nelson was too busy to waste his time on puff pieces, now that he was the network's lead investigative journalist.

Laney couldn't help but beam with pride every time she thought of it. After much encouragement, Paul had finally put his foot down with the network: Let him report on the stories he wanted to, or he was going to walk. He had a successful career as a uVer to fall back on, and he wasn't afraid to branch out on his own.

And despite his anxiety over it, the network had agreed. Of course, it hadn't hurt matters that Paul's investigative work had led to the arrest of the two women at the head of a ring of art thieves that had hit dozens of museums across the United States. Suzette and Seleste Cherniske were now serving time for grand larceny, arson, and aggravated assault. Though they would likely eventually be paroled, Laney was sure it would be a cold day in the Sahara before either of them showed their faces around here again.

Over the weeks that had followed the showdown in The Dalles, Laney had learned that Seleste had, in fact, been a highly talented artist who had never had success selling her own work. However, in her business as a restorer, she'd soon realized her talent for forgery was an even more valuable skill. With Suze to help her target museums across the country, the sisters had done very well for themselves... until the day that brownie drew Laney's attention to the painting in the hall.

A glimmer above her head made Laney glance up. Two sprites were playing in the upper branches of the yew tree behind Viv. It had been two years, but Laney still couldn't quite get used to *Seeing* so clearly. She'd missed out on so much, just by being stubborn.

Not just with the fae. With everything. Absently, she twisted the ring on her left hand.

In the aftermath of the fire, Laney had been horrified to hear that Suze's house had been one of the homes destroyed by the flames. Rumor had it that the house didn't just burn, it *exploded*. The gossip line of Foreston had speculated that the cache of art supplies she stored in the house had made it extra combustible. But Laney had been crushed by the notion that the stolen paintings had been lost forever.

Fortunately, it turned out that she'd had nothing to worry about. A short time later, police in Portland had conducted a search of Seleste's home and found a number of stolen paintings, including the two from the Paine museum, and evidence of a third forgery from the Paine collection already in progress. Suze had brought them from her house to Seleste's that Monday evening, before they left for The Dalles together. Despite her confidence that she could pin the thefts and the arson on Diane, she'd been uneasy enough to want to get all the evidence out of her house. The original paintings had been safely returned to the museum. Laney smiled every time she passed the Victorian lady's portrait and saw the tear in the corner.

"Laney!"

She glanced up to see Taryn leaning out the bridal room window, waving her over.

"Taryn, shut that!" Laney hissed, hurrying over. "Diane'll have a fit."

"Tell the heifer that the collections manager said it's okay," Claudia called from inside.

"Claudia, will you shut up?" Carmen said through gritted teeth.

Laney laughed, poking her head through the window. After Suze's arrest, the position of collections manager had been left vacant. Carmen was the obvious choice for the job, and Viv had happily offered her the position. Carmen now worked at the museum full-time, which kept her busy during the times that Josh was overseas.

"Well, what do you think?" Taryn asked, striking a pose as Laney leaned against the windowsill. She, Carmen, and Claudia were dressed in period-accurate flapper dresses in complementary shades of mint green, peach, and mauve.

"You look great," said Laney.

"I believe the phrase you're looking for is 'the bee's knees,'" Taryn corrected, and Laney snorted.

Behind her, Tucker started barking again. Laney glanced over her shoulder. "Oh, Paul's back," she said.

"Food!" Claudia sang, heading for the door.

"Whoa, whoa, freeze!" Laney yelled from the window. "You are not going anywhere near food in any of the clothes from the show! Did you try everything on?"

"Yes, your majesty," Taryn grumbled.

"Everything fit perfectly. My compliments to the designers," Carmen said.

"All right, you're dismissed. But remember what I said: No food near the clothes!"

"There better be chocolate scones left when we get out of here," Taryn grumbled as Carmen swung the revolving window shut and latched it.

By the time Laney made it back to the tent, the designers and volunteers were crowded around the cashier's table, which had become an impromptu brunch buffet. Paul had brought back a smorgasbord from the bakery—bagels, croissants, muffins, and, of course, the all-important chocolate scone. Laney grabbed a napkin and snatched one to set aside for Taryn.

A familiar set of arms wrapped around her from behind, and she grinned, leaning back into the embrace. "How's it going, love?" Paul asked, his breath warm on her cheek.

"Everything is on track. Doors open in about an hour and I think we're already mostly done with setup," Laney said.

"Looks like it's going to be a busy day."

"It's bound to be. We almost doubled our ticket sales from the last time we actually held the event." She wiped the back of her hand across her sweaty forehead. "This is just the calm before the storm. Once we start letting people in, it's going to be a madhouse."

"In that case," said Paul, "what's say you and I take a little break for some peace and quiet? Enjoy our 'calm before the storm.'"

Laney grinned. "Sounds like a fabulous idea."

They passed Matthew on their way out of the tent, trying to restrain Tucker, who was staring longingly at the buffet table.

"For Taryn," Laney said, slapping the scone into her brother's hand.

"Thanks. Like I don't already have my hands full," Matthew said sarcastically.

"Take him for a walk down the trail!" Laney said.

"I can't. You know he's afraid of the woods," Matthew said.

Laney snorted. That dog really was afraid of everything.

The sound of human voices faded as they made their way down the path, the trees enveloping them. Soon, there was nothing but the rustle of leaves, the burbling water of the creek, and the sound of *other* voices, that only Laney could hear. Across the way, she spotted Bob deadheading a voluminous coral rosebush. She couldn't hear him, but she could see his lips moving. Talking to himself, or so it appeared. But Laney could see, now, the soft golden shimmer of the gnome on his shoulder.

Bob still wouldn't tell her what his faery blessing was. But Laney thought she might know. Bob spoke to the fae, and the fae seemed to speak back. Laney's theory was that Bob's faery blessing might be the ability to understand the fae's language—and if so, he might have the best gift the fae had ever bestowed.

Then the trees closed in around them, and there was nothing but her and Paul, her hand in his, her head on his shoulder.

They stopped at the clearing where the hollow tree stood. Here, on this spot, three months ago, they'd been married. It had been a small ceremony, with just their immediate family—Paul's parents and older brother had flown in from England—with a larger reception following in one of the estate's formal gardens. The tree had been blooming, a cascade of beautiful white flowers, just as it had that fateful night two years ago.

Paul drew Laney close, into the shade of the tree's living limbs, a canopy of green leaves. "Do you remember all those years ago when you told me about this place?" he asked, resting his forehead against hers.

"Of course," Laney replied. "I promised you I'd show it to you someday."

"That you did. But I certainly never imagined under what circumstances."

"You say that every time," Laney murmured, tipping her chin up to catch his lips with hers. He pulled her closer, his hand cupping her cheek, the breeze playing softly with her hair.

Everything was perfect.

Above their heads came a sound like a Steller's Jay, cackling with mirth. They drew apart, looking up into the branches above them. "There's a wood sprite watching us," Laney said.

Paul cocked his head, trying to follow Laney's gaze. "Is it laughing?"

Laney just smiled.

Author's Note

Unlike most of the settings of the Northwest Magic series, Foreston, Washington is not a real town. The reason I decided to diverge from reality a bit in this book is because of the subject matter. A forest fire factors prominently into the plot of the book, and I definitely did not want to threaten a real town with a destructive event like that, even fictionally! There have been several major fires in the western US and Canada in the recent past, including in the Columbia River Gorge on both sides of the Oregon-Washington border, and the wounds of lost homes, lost landmarks, and lost loved ones—due to the fires or complications from smoke inhalation—are still very raw and personal.

That said, while the setting and events are fictional, this book is drawn in many ways from real experiences. The fall of 2017 was a very stressful time for me due to the proximity of the Eagle Creek Fire to my home in Oregon and then the massively destructive Tubbs Fire in Sonoma County, California, where I went to college and where many of my friends still live. Because of their impact on my home regions past and present, preventing wildfires is very important to me. If you're interested in fire prevention, check out the National Fire Prevention Association's Firewise USA® program at Firewise.org.

Acknowledgments

Old Flames had an interesting journey to publication. It was originally intended to be a short prequel novella to the Northwest Magic series (hence the odd chronology of the series—*Old Flames* taking place two years before the first book in the series and sandwiched between it and *Fool's Gold*, the sequel that was foreshadowed in *Alexandra's Riddle*, which will now be the *third* book in the series), but the storyline just wasn't fitting with the rest of the series. There wasn't enough magic and there was no mystery... and if you know me, it's not an Elisa book if there's not a mystery in it! So I want to say thank you to my fellow romance author Jane Watson for your help brainstorming this story and transforming it into a full-fledged member of the Northwest Magic series. Jane saved my bacon not once, but twice on this book. I had been stuck for months because the story wasn't clicking the way I wanted it to. I'm so glad we managed to work through it!

Thank you to my editor, Rose Anne Roper; to my dear friend and beta reader, Emily Davies, for your help with Britishisms; to my cover designer, Najla Qamber, and her team; to everyone at

Crimson Fox Publishing, particularly Clare Dugmore, for all your help; to my assistant, Esther Hadassah, for holding everything together; and to Lynnette Yoder, for your prayers about my writers' block (they worked!).

Thank you to my readers for your patience and all your support while I figured out how to make this book what it needed to be.

Thank you to my family for everything you do for me.

And thank You to God for getting me through this difficult season. I was convinced I would never write again, but You told me to be still and wait.

About the Author

Elisa Keyston is an author of sweet romance with hints of magic, intrigue, and suspense. She was the series lead for the first season of The Pioneer Brides of Rattlesnake Ridge, a shared-world historical romance series from Sweet Promise Press, and she's also the author of the Northwest Magic series from Crimson Fox Publishing, a sweet contemporary romance series with a touch of magic and mystery set in her home state of Oregon. She's a graduate of Sonoma State University with a degree in history, which inspired her love of historical fiction and modern stories set in historic places. When she's not writing, Elisa spends most of her time gardening, collecting gnomes and fairies for her backyard, and fawning over her furbabies. Visit Elisa online and sign up for her newsletter at elisakeyston.com.

Other Books by the Author

NORTHWEST MAGIC

Alexandra's Riddle

Fool's Gold (coming soon)

THE PIONEER BRIDES OF RATTLESNAKE RIDGE

Arriving from Arkansas